Ac...

ROSES & BONES

Praise for PSYCHE IN A DRESS:

"Block deftly weaves myth and magic into scenes from contemporary life, viewed through a shimmering prism of the very hip." —*Publishers Weekly* (starred review)

"Riveting and brilliant, this is a must for most YA collections." —*SLJ*

"A sort of fevered dream written in Block's unique, darkly evocative style." —*KLIATT*

"Vignettes of urgent free verse make for a fast read. Block raises the edgy question: 'Is beauty monstrous?'" —ALA *Booklist*

"An illusory, though emotionally realistic, world that is both ethereal and edgy." —*Kirkus Reviews*

Praise for ECHO:

"Echo begs not just to be read, but to be reread, and savored." —*Publishers Weekly* (starred review)

"The sorceress of iridescent language is back again." —*Kirkus Reviews*

"Evocative. Block weaves a spell over readers ready to enter her universe."   —*KLIATT*

"Block has a penchant for transformative, kaleidoscopic language, and there are moments of sheer exhilaration in the words combined herein."   —*BCCB*

"References and allusions to Shakespeare and *The Wizard of Oz* commingle in the strange, tantalizing mix that is Block's trademark."   —*The Horn Book*

Praise for THE ROSE AND THE BEAST:

"Block uses language like a jeweled sword, glittering as it cuts to the heart."   —*Kirkus Reviews* (starred review)

"Intoxicating. Heady. The darkness of the conflicts and subjects proves the strength of the magic Block describes: the transfiguring power of love."

—*Publishers Weekly* (starred review)

"Block's lush, beautiful words turn modern-day Los Angeles into a fantastical world of fairies, angels, and charms."

—ALA *Booklist*

"Block's Beauty and Beast step into the rose garden and turn popular romance into metaphysical mystery. Angela Carter and Emma Donoghue have ventured this way before; their fans will eagerly accompany Block on her journey through this dark but magic mirror." —*BCCB*

"Block's style is almost more poetry than prose as she interweaves contemporary life with common themes without losing the timeless feel; the stories could be happening anywhere, and to anyone." —*SLJ*

ROSES & BONES

ALSO BY FRANCESCA LIA BLOCK:

Weetzie Bat

Missing Angel Juan

Girl Goddess #9: Nine Stories

The Hanged Man

Dangerous Angels: The Weetzie Bat Books

I Was a Teenage Fairy

Violet and Claire

Guarding the Moon

Wasteland

Goat Girls: Two Weetzie Bat Books

Beautiful Boys: Two Weetzie Bat Books

Necklace of Kisses

Blood Roses

How to (Un)cage a Girl

The Waters & the Wild

Pretty Dead

The Frenzy

House of Dolls

ROSES & BONES

Myths, Tales, and Secrets

A collection of three books by

FRANCESCA LIA BLOCK

HARPER TEEN

An Imprint of HarperCollinsPublishers

FOR GILDA, JASMINE, AND SAM

Book One
PSYCHE IN A DRESS
Page 1

Book Two
ECHO
Page 115

Book Three
THE ROSE AND THE BEAST
Page 265

ROSES & BONES

PSYCHE IN A DRESS

Psyche

I AM NOT A GODDESS

I am my father's

My father had me mutilated twice
He had my mother and sisters murdered more than once
but he has never killed me off
sometimes I think he only gave me life
so I could be his muse, his actress

They say he does things with me
to work through issues he had with my mother
I look just like her in the early films but
now she is gone

In the first film I had to take off my top
I stood there, shivering
with my hands covering my breasts
as the cameras were rolling
A million caterpillars crawled over my bones
and my stomach was filled with the wings of dying moths
But I knew what I had to do

I am an actress
I am my father's
I do my job

It was easier after that
I got used to all the crew watching
My father watching
People said that I was odd-looking
not the typical face you see
but my father tells me I am perfect, just what he wants
My father says
"These actors, they try to do too much
You know how to just be
Don't try to do anything else

You are an actress
My princess"

I live with my father
in a dirty-white mansion
made of the bones and teeth of actors
It has been the scene of many atrocities
in my father's films
There are crumbling columns in front
and a dining room we never use
with a giant chandelier from which
one of my father's characters hung herself
There is a huge tiled pool
surrounded by crumbling, headless, limbless statues
ficus trees entwined with morning glories
beds of calla lilies
and oleander bushes
I can see the pool from my window
empty
my father rarely fills it with water
It was used for a drowning in another film
I have a large room

with a large bed draped in diaphanous fabrics
I have my own bathroom with a sunken tub and a view
through glass walls
of my private, somewhat overgrown rose garden
peeling white iron chairs and mossy fountains
I have a walk-in closet of my mother's designer clothes
In one interview I read
my mother said that she sold her soul for that wardrobe
A black satin-trimmed smoking jacket and trousers
a white satin-trimmed smoking jacket and matching satin
skirt, a golden pleated chiffon Grecian gown, a golden
sweater covered with gemstones, a white silk wrap
dress covered with giant red peonies, a pink suit with a
short jacket and skirt, shift dresses in white, black, red
sapphire, emerald and tangerine silk or satin, some
with large bows in back, piles of cashmere sweaters
in lipstick colors, some with silk flowers from obis
appliquéd on them, and many, many shoes

When my mother left us, she took only a black suit
a pair of jeans, a red silk blouse
her jewels and five pairs of the shoes

Sometimes I lie awake at night
wondering how she chose them
I knew which ones they were
because I knew her wardrobe better than she did:
black leather riding boots
black lizard pumps
strappy golden sandals
ruby red flats
emerald green satin dancing shoes with ankle straps
I was so jealous of those shoes
Sometimes I put on one of the dresses
light candles
and dance with my mother's shadow
Most of the time, at night, I use only candles in my room
waiting for her to come back
Even a wraith is better than nothing
even a silhouette on the wall

My father's new girlfriend, Aphrodite
wanted to be the star of his film
and he wouldn't replace me
Once I heard him saying to her, "She's seventeen!

She's seventeen!
What do you expect?"
Enraging her even more
They screamed at each other all night
Until the chandelier shattered
And a thousand swallows flew through the open window
whirring their wings
In the morning she was gone
but she was not finished

One night I was lying in my bed
wearing an antique cotton nightgown
white as a bride
My father was out drinking with his producer
It was completely dark
Not even the candles were lit
I could have been abandoned
on a mountaintop—
the wind in my chest
was that cold
That was when you came
Through the open window

with the night-blooming jasmine
that grows up the old stone garden wall
You knelt beside my bed and put your head near mine
You whispered, "I just want to lie beside you tonight
I won't hurt you"

I was afraid at first
Lay very still, waiting for pain
It felt like a scene from one of my father's movies
The killer with the beautiful voice
For a moment I wondered
if my father had staged the whole thing
If he had a camera somewhere?
I wouldn't put it past him

You only talked to me
You said, "Tell me"
You asked, "Do you think Love and Soul are the same?
If not, how does the Soul earn Love?
How does Love find his Soul?
Can one exist without the other?
If Love and the Soul had a child

what would her name be?"

"Tell me your name," I said
"You already know
If you are Soul
I am the other one"

I heard the sea in your voice—
sheer waves breaking on pale powdered sand
I heard the glossy rustlings of the cypress and olive trees—
the footsteps of maenads and panpipes playing
echoing caves in the mountains—
cloven hooves striking the rock
At their approach birds took flight into the white skies
After a long time I fell asleep

In the morning you were gone

But you came
again and again
I asked to see you but you said
that was the one rule

I couldn't put on
the light
Even so, I asked you to lie beside me
After a while I reached out
and held your hand
"I'm so crazy," I said
"What's wrong with me?
You come through my window at night
I haven't seen your face
And I want you"

Even in darkness
your lips taste of sunshine
They leave a slight stinging spray on my lips
Your skin melts over me
I feel you enter like a shaft of light
My bones dissolve around you
We become liquid, eternal
I am released
from my mortality

You wiped my body with a cool towel

I told you what my father shot today
You said, "If you were my daughter
I would just sit you in front of a camera
and let it watch your face for hours, every expression"
"He cut off my mother's head," I said
"He made it keep talking
She had to have a mask made of her face
plaster and bandages
She is claustrophobic
and she said she almost died
breathing through those little straws"

You held me in your arms
and pressed your lips against my hair
After a long time you whispered
"The wild girls cut off Orpheus's head
He shouldn't have looked behind him
His music could have brought
Eurydice back from the dead"

"But he didn't hear her footsteps," I said

"You can't doubt your gifts"

"Maybe he didn't doubt himself
Maybe he doubted her, his love for her"

You were quiet, thinking

"My father doesn't doubt," I said

"What about you?"

I shook my head
Doubt tastes like sand in the mouth

"Philomela was raped
and her tongue cut out so she wouldn't tell
She turned into a nightingale and sang
her story"

You told me all the myths, one after the other
night after night
my beautiful, brutal bedtime tales

As you spoke I closed my eyes and saw them come to life
the miniature figures acting out their parts
When we fell asleep
my dreams were more vivid than they had ever been
As if I were watching your dreams in my head—

The man who got to be a flower with a hundred petals
admiring himself in a pool forever
while the girl who loved him was only a voice
unable even to choose her words
The girl who crashed through the earth
in a chariot drawn by black steeds
punished for just one red pomegranate seed
unable to choose where she lived
a queen
only in darkness
a princess, her mother's daughter
weaker
in the light

Love's mother, the jealous one
who sent his beloved on a quest

carrying her heart in her hands
like a broken urn
Love the shining god with wings
Love the monster

"I love you," I said
"Please let me
see you"
And you said, "You can't doubt so much, Psyche"
But my half sisters were wearing black dresses
and big sunglasses
Their skin was tan
They came to visit me
I heard their heels click wickedly on the marble floor
"Tell us about this lover of yours"
"There isn't anybody"
"Bullshit," my oldest sister said
"Your skin never looked so good"
They wouldn't stop asking

"I've never seen him," I told them finally
"What?"

They were appalled
"He only comes at night"
"You've never seen his face?"

He smells like night-blooming flowers
Crushed, juicy petals on the pillows
His voice is full of ocean
Humming like the surf
He kneels before me like I am his goddess
He is a god

They laughed at me
Then their faces turned
grave
"You must make him show himself," they said
"He may be a monster"

Why did I listen to them?
They have long white-blonde hair
large breasts
and brown skin
like their mother

I have my mother's black hair, blue eyes and pale skin
full features and large hands like my father
My breasts are small with large aureoles
my legs long and too thin
I know there is something odd
in the way my knees touch and my neck strains
I am not sure why you chose me
Maybe you are a monster?

One night you came to me
I hid in the shadows and waited
I saw a dark figure go to the bed
feel around for the shape of my body
Your movements became more agitated
when you did not find me
You called my name
lay down on the sheets and searched for my scent
moved restlessly for a while like a baby or an animal
and then became
very still
I crept over to you and lit the candle I held
It was a tall taper that smelled of melting honey

In its light my lover was revealed

Is beauty monstrous?
If so, then my sisters were right
His beauty was so sharp it could have cut
out my heart
He lay naked, sleeping on my bed
How could it be?
Why had he chosen me?
I wanted to run and hide from him

As I stood, amazed, a drop of wax from the candle fell
and touched his bare shoulder
He cried out and leapt up
His face filled with pain

"I told you not to look at me," he said
"My mother was right"

No girl wants to hear those words

He was so bright, a conflagration
And I

I had seen too much
I had seen the god
I was not
a goddess
I dropped to my knees and covered my eyes
"Don't come back here," I said

"Why do you doubt so much, Psyche?"

He reached to touch my shoulder but I pulled away
And then he was gone

My room has never been so empty
There is only one monster
Here
She is ready to do anything to be forgiven
She has been mutilated
(On film, but still)
Her mother has been murdered more than once
Now the monster's mother is just gone
What more must monster girl do to find the god again?

Echo

THE FILM MY FATHER PUT ME IN WAS CALLED *NARCISSUS*
He saw that I was broken
and he thought it might work well for his next project

I went to the set without any makeup
The ladies frowned at my skin
turned my face this way and that
in the harsh lights

"What are you eating?" they asked me
"Dairy? Sugar?"
"Do you get any sleep?"
"Supplements? Facials?"
"You've got to start taking care of yourself"

I shrugged
I said I was okay
I had just inherited my father's complexion
And now of course
I didn't have the benefit of sex with a god every night

At least in this film no one gets raped, mutilated
or murdered
Unless you count vanishing as murder
It's what you assume in this world these days
when someone
disappears
I was supposed to vanish
turn into a voice

Narcissus came to the first reading late
He didn't apologize
My father didn't say anything
Anyone else
he'd have fired on the spot
Instead he just scowled
at me

I turned away so he couldn't see

Narcissus had long, gold ringlets
chiseled features
and a body like a temple
Don't look too deeply into his eyes, though
You will never find your reflection

I'll probably be fine if he doesn't touch me
I told myself
But that was not my father's plan

Narcissus and I went out for dinner
My father set it up
There was a bar of red-veined marble
with spigots spurting wine like blood
Stargazer lilies stained the white linen tablecloths
with their rusty powder
A woman was covertly nibbling the petals
The food had no scent
Beautiful people sat staring at themselves in the mirrors
Their twins emerged out of glass pools

to have sex with them on the tabletops
In the candlelight I wondered
if Narcissus might find me attractive
Not that I cared
Love had already left me

I had on makeup and a blue satin chinoiserie dress
my mother's jewels—
a double strand of pearls and her sapphire ring
I imagined her teeth, her eyes

I asked Narcissus about himself
I didn't expect him to say anything interesting
but when he started talking I fell
under his spell
Instead of touching parts of my mother
I watched Narcissus's full lips move over *his* white teeth
His eyes were pools shattered by sunlight
and his lashes brushed his cheekbones
If he was looking at his reflection
I couldn't see

Narcissus

NARCISSUS LIVED WITH HIS MOTHER IN AN
apartment on a street lined with other apartments that
looked just like it—a cottage cheese stucco-and-glass
building with a pool in the center.

Narcissus swam alone late at night with his reflection.
The pool made everything blue, including Narcissus's skin.
The air always smelled of chlorine. When Narcissus swam
it got into his hair so he washed carefully with his mother's
expensive shampoo before he went to sleep.

After school, Narcissus took the bus to the beach where
he went surfing or perfected his tan. When he got home
his mother was never there. He defrosted his dinner and
went into the bathroom paneled with mirrors. He took off

his clothes and admired his abdominal muscles, his skin, his cock.

Narcissus's father had left before he could remember. His mother was not there. She said she was an actress but Narcissus suspected something else because there were never any roles he knew of but always enough money, heavy makeup, tight dresses, the stink of men. Narcissus never wanted to smell like that.

When he talked to her she looked right through him if she looked his way at all. But suddenly he had discovered, in those mirrors, someone even more beautiful. Someone completely devoted. Someone who would never look away.

A lot of people didn't look away. There were women and men wanting sexual favors. But Narcissus stopped caring about them. It was easier to stand in front of the mirrors, caressing himself.

Sometimes his twin would materialize. Cold as glass and without a smell but so beautiful that it didn't matter. They could fuck all night, tireless, insatiable, exactly the same.

One day on the boardwalk a tall, thin man with pale skin, a hat and dark glasses approached Narcissus. The man seemed out of place and spoke with a thick accent. He handed Narcissus his card and said, "Have you ever acted before?"

Narcissus smiled because in some ways that was all he had ever done. "Why?" he asked.

"I am making a film," the man said. "I need someone to help make my daughter disappear."

"DO YOU KNOW WHAT I LIKE ABOUT YOU, ECHO?"

Narcissus said
"You know how to listen
Most of these actresses I know
just want to go on and on about themselves"

Perhaps this, too, was a test
Narcissus did not taste of the spray
that spurts from the skin of ripe oranges
When we touched it was for the cameras
His pupils were blank
empty
My reflection was never there
The lights were bright, revealing the monsters
He watched himself the whole time

"Who are you?" Narcissus's character asked
"You . . . you . . . you"

Those were my lines
I went home and looked in the giant tarnished mirror
with the frame of silver roses
I had not vanished
I had not faded
away to just a voice
Maybe I wish I had
It was my voice that had been stolen away

Eurydice

STRAY DOGS FOLLOWED ORPHEUS THROUGH THE STREETS
feral cats crawled onto his lap
wild parrots flew down to light
upon his shoulders
rolling their eyes in ecstasy
eucalyptus trees swooned when he passed them
jacarandas did a striptease of purple petals

Orpheus tapped the mike
and squinted out into the audience
shifting the weight of his narrow hips
He cleared his throat
but it still sounded like he'd just had a cigarette

He ran his hand through his hair, slicking it back
sang a cappella
with his hands in the back pockets of his jeans
leaning into the microphone as if he were going to go
down on it
then played his guitar
Music can make a man a demigod
especially to a girl who has seen Love
up close
and burned
and lost him
especially to a girl without a voice
I had never understood the expression
about your heart being in your mouth
It beat there, choking me with blood

After the last song he came off the stage
and someone introduced us
I could see the dark roots of his bleached hair
The insomniac circles under his eyes
He had the irises of a mystic
Pale, almost fanatical

His voice was gravelly
His hands were warm with large blue veins
I could hear incantations in his blood
"I've seen your films," he said
"I'd like to talk with you more some time"

The next night we ate avocados, oranges and honey
in Orpheus's candlelit cavern deep in the canyon
I wore strapless pale lace and tulle and lilies in my hair
"Tell me," he said
"Tell me a story"
This in itself was an aphrodisiac
My throat opened like a flower

He listened to the myths
The ones my love once gave me
Orpheus liked their darkness and the violence
and the truth
For me it is the transformation

I was restless, sweating in my dress
"Let's go," I said, "Let's go, O"

We ran out into the canyon
Up the hillsides to the street
The sky was bright, hallucinatory, pink
We ran into the neighborhood of rotting mansions
When the sun set we roamed their damp lawns
kissed under the purple trees
There was a pink restaurant with a green awning
We broke inside and explored the shadowy booths
the cobwebs draping the bar
We waltzed on the dance floor with ghosts of dead stars
When the sun rose we ate waffles with whipped cream
in an all-night coffee shop
Sunshine burned through the glass
searing the night off our skins
Back in his cavern, Orpheus sang my myths to me
I imagined that I would stop telling stories
stop acting in my father's films
I would give up my aspirations
I do not need to be an artist, I told myself
I do not need to be a goddess
I will be a woman, a wife, a muse

But this is what I could not give up:

I could not give up myself

And my self had become

the memory of the god who once visited me each night

I could not give up the chance to win him back

How could I win him back if I were happy with another?

It would never happen.

I would need to prove myself, suffer

I would need the god

of hell

Orpheus

ORPHEUS WAS A MUSICAL PRODIGY. WHAT ELSE,
*with a name like that? In another place and time his mother
might have been a muse of epic poetry, but in this world
of separation she was only a woman afraid of poverty and
growing old. She took all the money her son made from his
first album and bought a small mansion with etched-glass
windows, gold columns and a spiked gate. She bought a car
and furs and jewels for herself, new breasts. In another place
and time, Orpheus's father might have been the sun god, or
at least a king, but instead he was a frightened, bankrupt
man who never told Orpheus's mother to stop what she was
doing.*

Orpheus refused to play music for anyone. He locked

*himself in his room and wrote silent poetry in his journals.
He could hear the song of it, his secret. Orpheus's mother
knocked on the door, wanting another album, more money
for new skin—on her face, another fur coat. That was when
he left the fancy house that he had paid for with music. He
never spoke to either of his parents again.*

*Orpheus went wandering through the canyons. He
found secret underground passageways, crumbling caverns
where he hid, got high, smoked packs of cigarettes. One
night he ventured out and played his guitar for the birch
trees. They danced in the moonlight, their many dark eyes
watching, pale silver skin quivering. In the morning the
avocado and citrus trees filled his open palms with fruit.
Overblown orange poppies with opiate seeds grew out of
the parched dirt. Bees let him reach his bare hands into
their hives, scooping out gobs of honey, unstung. Rabbits,
squirrels and doves gathered to listen to this new Orpheus,
the magician, the mystic, realizing his truth, even in a time
without muses, kings or sun gods.*

*It was hard to live on avocados and oranges, and when
the tobacco and pot ran out Orpheus got a job as a bar-
tender in a seedy strip club and sang onstage after hours.*

The strippers were like birch trees, he found—that silvery and wide-eyed, that susceptible to his charms. He slept with a lot of them. But when he met Eurydice he knew he wanted more. Alone in his cavern, with the insatiable dancing trees awaiting him, he wanted a wife.

When Eurydice left him the maenad came. She wanted more than a husband.

AFTER ORPHEUS BEGAN TO DOUBT

he could not reclaim me

If you are to love, never look back
I should have told him
But what do I know?
I am just as filled with doubt
I am only Eurydice
I am known as Orpheus's
I was never a goddess

My father didn't argue with me when I said I had to leave
He smiled to himself
"Whatever you want, princess
You'll be back in time"

I went away to a new city
and half waited for Orpheus to come for me

To lead me back with his poetry

Dear Orpheus, why did you doubt?
You are an artist
When you sing your words
all the women want your child in their bellies
All the men want to stand where you stand
The god of hell should not intimidate you

Orpheus did not come
Days and days passed
I lived in the tall, cold building
I put on the stray pieces I had brought
from my mother's wardrobe
and walked to school bent under the weight of my books
I sat in the echoing lecture halls
and listened for the poetry hidden
in the professors' words
But I couldn't hear it
I ate but the food had no taste
I drank the alcohol
that was given out every night at the parties

I watched my belly bloat and my face break out
Someone offered me acid
but when I looked out my window
eight flights to the ground below
I knew I couldn't take it
It would have been too easy to jump

I wondered if Orpheus was writing about me
I wondered if I was getting closer to hell

My sister called me and said
"Did you hear? Are you okay?"
"Hear what?" I asked
but I knew it was bad

"You know he was dating that crazy singer?
They were doing heroin.
Something happened. Orpheus is dead."

Love had left again
I had no doubts about hell now
I was all the way there

The Maenad

THE MAENAD'S FATHER TOLD HER SHE WAS *stupid, a slut. She took off her clothes and danced in the snow, hoping it would make her skin that perfect, white and untouched. But as soon as she stepped into it, the frost became dirty sludge. Her lips were red bitten blood. The roots of her hair were black like the branches that scratched her arms. She wrote poetry and played her guitar so she wouldn't have to cut herself with something sharper than wood, the fingers of trees. Her guitar spoke and lay in her arms but was not warm. She was only looking for someone to love her.*

The maenad went to the big faraway city and formed a band. She threw herself around the stage, whipping her

neck, flashing her breasts, bruising her hipbones, spin-
ning until the world whirled away. Oh, obliterating ec-
stasy. When she opened her eyes she spit into the audience,
thinking the boys with the beefy faces were her father.

After the shows she was starving, bloodless. She de-
voured meat, imagining she was ingesting the flesh of the
god of pleasure and pain, becoming one with him, divine.
She drank wine, imagining it was that same god's blood,
the god of the beautiful and the cruel.

And Orpheus, he was like a limb of that god. When she
heard him sing she felt herself changing. When she touched
him she felt herself becoming powerful, beautiful, pure.
They ate wild narcotic poppies in his cavern while the bees
and lovesick birch trees clamored outside; they wanted
him as much as she did.

"Don't close your eyes," she wailed.

She didn't want him to leave her, even for a moment.
Even in his dreams.

She asked him, "Do you still love that girl?"

He said it was over.

The maenad knew the only way she could be sure was
to do something irreversible, terrible, mythic.

AND YOU CAME

hell god

At a concert downtown

Somewhere dark, I don't remember

The air hissed with sound

The chandeliers were shattering

Black smoke swirled around the stage

I sat on the ground

in the pool

of my mother's old aqua blue taffeta dress

I wore rhinestones on my breasts and on my ears

I wore black gloves with the fingers cut out

black satin pointy-toed stilettos like a wicked bird

Bees swarmed around me, buzzing in my ears

I had a forked tongue and horns and a tail

I saw you and I said, that is the one for me

My hair caught fire

You took me home
It was an old Victorian building
wooden floor painted black—
so shiny, a lake—
no furniture except the low black lacquer bed and table
You kissed me until I passed over
The corpse of my body
was stuffed with black lilies and buzzing bees

I forgot Orpheus, my song
I even forgot my first lover, Love
I stopped wanting anything else in the world
We ran through the city
The air smelled of smoke
Pieces of ash rained down
Some headless mannequins
were lined up on the sidewalk by the trash
You put them in your hearse and took them home
In Chinatown the cloisonné vases
were covered with dust
The animals hung dead in the windows
We ate sticky noodles and pork buns with plum sauce

There was a sign next to a cage of chickens

THESE BIRDS TO EAT NOT FOR PETS

No one looked at us as we ran up and down the hills

The air smelled of burning meat

We were invisible

We were demons

I wanted my mother

I am not a goddess, I said

But you are a god

The god of chaos

The god of hell

Hades, my love

You are a businessman

You own a tattoo parlor

and a clothing store that sells leather clothes, masks

whips and handcuffs

sex toys and porn

You are a club promoter

We went to some kind of old mansion you had found

at the edge of the park

I was wearing my mother's white smoking jacket over her

tight black cocktail dress

and black satin shoes with sharp points

People were standing

around a pool

that you had filled with dry ice

Their drinks were a strange, smoky green

I wondered how absinthe tasted

as I ate my poisonous maraschino cherries

The band was playing in what had once been a ballroom

You had discovered them

They looked like birds of prey

and their music beat past me on dark wings

You had the room filled with chandeliers, broken

like crystallized tears

Thousands and thousands of dried leaves

blew through the corridors

Black hounds guarded the doors

Everyone said you were brilliant

Everyone said you were some kind of genius

We went to a small glass café overlooking the dark water

and drank something I didn't recognize
in the red leather booth
"You are corrupting me, my darling," I said
having another bittersweet sip

I felt my body melting under the table
The waves crashed against the rocks
What if I couldn't get up and leave?
Would you desert me here?
No, you took me home again
You bit me gently, not drawing blood
You fed me pomegranate seeds
I sucked the clear red coating off the sharp white pith
The taste was sweet at first
and then dry as dirt, as bone

"I love you so much that I don't care if I die," I told you
So what if you didn't say it back?
Your hair was always cold against my burning skin, cold
and smelled of smoke
Your skin was always cool and sleek
Hades, my love

Are you just one more task
to bring back the lover I burned with my candle wax?
with the flame of my doubt?

One day after we had eaten oranges in the rare sunlight
I remembered him
the pressure of his lips on my forehead
and at my throat—
making my hot skin feel icy with their burn
The calluses and soft places on his hands
The vibration of his voice in his chest
as he gave me the myths again
I told you the story then, and you said
"He was a monster to do that to you
Did he think he was so much better than you
that you couldn't see him?"

I told you about Orpheus and you said
"Maybe he didn't kill himself
Maybe his girlfriend shot him in the head"

You had different ways to bite
I wondered how much more pressure it would take
to make the blood come

Once we drove all the way back to the city I'm from
We passed the cattle waiting for slaughter
by the side of the highway
The air reeked with fear
You said you grew up on a farm
You saw cows killed
When I asked you to tell me more
about your childhood you just laughed
cranked up
the music and rammed
your foot against the pedal

We didn't stop in the city
but drove all the way through to the border
There were signs along the highway
of silhouetted, running people
holding the hands of their children
like animals, like targets

At the border you turned off the music

smoothed your hair with some water

from the bottle you had gripped between your thighs

You took off your sunglasses and spoke politely

"Yes, Officer, no sir"

No one would have suspected you

No one would have thought, This is Hades himself

In the border town the light was harsh

Dust motes looked as if they were catching on fire

You took my hand and we ran

through the unpaved streets, past the little shops

We bought loads of black leather belts

and cuffs studded with sharp silver

You pulled me down some stairs

into a dark bar where you made me drink tequila

I marveled at the worm saturated with poison

My head was pounding as we emerged

back up into the sun

A lovely girl had a huge tumor in her neck

A man was missing his hand

We found a punk band playing in the dust

The lead singer was a Mexican albino
with tattoos all over his body and shaved head
The band was good, really fast
You gave them your card and spoke to them in Spanish
I was so thirsty
We ate some greasy food and you ordered beers
There was a tiny building that said CASAMIENTOS
and you said we should get married
You laughed
and I felt like the worm in the tequila bottle—
bloated, sick, greenish-white, trapped, in love
That night there were fireworks
You grabbed my hand and we ran through the streets
as the sky exploded
There was panic in your eyes I didn't understand

Maybe I had imagined it
I was wearing my mother's green satin cocktail dress
hemmed short, above my knees
and dusty black cowboy boots
We headed back that night
and slept by the sea in your truck

I vomited on the sand
You carried me into the ocean as the sun rose
"Good for hangovers," you said
I was so cold
I didn't stop shivering for hours after I got out
The sun turned the water to aluminum foil
I was afraid it would all just burn up
anyway

Then suddenly you stopped wanting me
You turned away
You wouldn't touch me
I lay staring at your cold, muscular white back
your blue-black shiny hair
I wondered what I had done wrong—
I had lost weight, so my belly was concave again
I was seeing a dermatologist—
Or maybe I was being selfish
Maybe you had been wounded when you were younger
Maybe you had been damaged and this wasn't about me
at all

I tried to ask you if you had been hurt
"Do you know Philomela?" I asked
"Who?"
"The myth
She was raped by her sister's husband
When she threatened to tell, he cut out her tongue
She turned into a nightingale
She sang her story"

"Do you want to know why we don't have sex?"
you asked
I started to cry and you said
"Not everyone has been molested, okay?
Maybe I just don't want to fuck you anymore.
Have you ever thought of that?"
"Is there something I could do differently?" I asked
"We could try it different ways," I said
You smiled at me
Your incisors sharp
Your eyes were two dark bandages
"I thought you'd never ask, baby," you said

The more punishment, the sooner I will be redeemed?
You had finally earned your name.

Hades

HADES GREW UP ON A FARM IN AN OLD RED
house next to a dilapidated barn. *There were cornfields
stretching to the horizon; maybe they went on forever.
Hades believed they were haunted. The wind in the corn
sang strange whispers. Sometimes he'd catch glimpses of
emaciated people, thin as scarecrows, with corncob pipes,
straw hats, missing teeth, wading shoulder deep through
the cornfields. Sometimes he imagined he heard children
screaming.*

*Once at baseball practice he was almost struck by light-
ning. It hit a tree beside him instead, charred and gnarled
it, and he kept imagining his own body ruined like that.*

In the winter it was so cold that Hades got frostbite.

He had stayed out too late in the snow making angels, not wanting to return home. His father told him he might lose his fingers. He lay in bed trying not to cry, imagining the stumps on his hands.

In the summer Hades was always bathed in sweat from the humidity. His mother screamed at him to bathe. "You stink!" At night he ran through the meadows catching fireflies in jars. Then he took them home and watched them die, the lights snuffed out.

He saw animals born and he saw them slaughtered. Blood was just something that was on your hands all the time. Blood was just another bodily fluid. There were more interesting ones.

When Hades wet his bed at the age of five his mother put him back in diapers. She stuck the pins into him. She kept diapering him until he was twelve years old.

When Hades had an erection his mother locked him in the closet. Sometimes she even beat him. This didn't stop Hades from getting hard. It made him harder in every way.

Hades's father waited for him when he came out of the shower. He commented on the size of Hades's penis. He *showed his son his own. There was something odd about the way Hades's father taught him to slaughter a cow. There was some kind of pleasure in it. Sometimes Hades's father would set off fireworks from behind the barn and watch to see his son jump at the noise.*

Hades's mother did not like how her husband looked at their son. Because of this she beat Hades even harder. She beat him and locked him in the closet and finally Hades left home.

He had been born an unscarred, sweet-smelling baby with pale down on his head that soon fell out and blue eyes that turned pupil-less black. He had been born loving animals and tractors, getting lost in the lightning bug meadows, lost in the angel-making snow. He had become something else entirely. So he decided to become something else again. He changed his name, he changed the color of his hair, he wore eyeliner and grew his fingernails, changed his skin with ink tattoos of devil girls. He went alone into the desert to set off fireworks to immunize himself to loud sounds. He developed an insatiable appetite for meat, any food that bled, that had once had eyes. He became rich, a businessman. He listened to the loudest music, sought it out, to further immunize himself.

Hades saw Eurydice and plucked her like a flower. He became for her the god of chaos, the god of hell. This was why he wanted her. She was proof of his success, his change.

Persephone

AT LAST, SHE CAME FOR ME
I had waited forever

I took the train home from my hell god
It was late morning
My mouth was parched
My skin felt raw
My eyes ached in the sunlight
There were bruises and bite marks
hidden under my clothes
One of my ribs was dislocated
I heard it pop out when Hades took me from behind
and every time I breathed

I felt the scrape of it

I did not think of myself as damaged, as a victim
I saw myself as a woman in love
I had forgotten that this was just maybe another trial
another task I must accomplish
another test

She was waiting for me in the lobby of the building
where I lived
Someone had let her in
She had slept all night on the horrible, scratchy sofa
She had gained weight and she had wrinkles
and she was so beautiful to me
I wanted to jump back inside of her
That was all I could think of

She didn't say anything, she just held me
I wept into her long white linen trench coat
My rib hurt more when I cried but I didn't care
She smelled like wildflowers, and that is not the same
as other flowers but much lighter—

a little acrid and sun-warmed and windy
She wore beautiful Italian shoes and no jewels

We went to the hotel where she was staying
It was a small villa overlooking the city
She ordered room service—
poached eggs under a silver cover, smoked salmon,
fruit and cheese, sparkling water
She made me take a bath
using the tiny bottle of green bath gel
and the soft white washcloth
When I came out
wrapped in the white terry cloth bathrobe
we sat on the bed and ate our meal
I realized how hungry I was

"How did you find me?" I asked her
"Your father"
"You went to him?
I thought you were never going to talk to him again"
"Everything was dying," my mother said
"I was killing it; I couldn't help myself

Without you everything was dead
and I knew I had to see him again
To find you
Anything was worth finding you"
"What did he make you do?" I asked
I knew my father. He didn't do things for free
"Oh, nothing, don't worry, darling," she said
"Eat your eggs"
It was dark in the room
The pale green drapes were drawn closed
The sounds of the city were soft, faraway below us

"Now, who did this to you?"
She put her hand on my rib cage
Her fingers felt so good there, so cool
"What do you mean?"
"I'm not naïve, you know
Remember who I married?
I see all the signs"
I shook my head
"It's not like that"
I didn't want to tell her about Hades

Or even Orpheus
I wanted to tell her about my first lover, Love
The one who never hurt me
He killed me but he never
hurt me
Do you understand?

"I know that you are here with the god of hell," my
mother said calmly. "I know because for me everything
is dying. I want you to come back with me so I can come
back to life. We can live together. You can go to school
there. This place is terrible for you. Look at you."

But it wasn't as simple
as that
What if I returned with her
and left my god of darkness?
Would I ever grow up?
Would I ever pass the test?
Would my first lover be mine again?
No, I would stay
a strange little girl, living with her mother

until they both died in some ritual
holding on to each other
the flowers blooming around them
killing them with beauty

"I can't," I told her
"It's more complicated"
"Let's go out," my mother said
as if she wanted to show me
that the beauty of the world would not destroy me
That it was ours

The sun had come out and the city smelled of flowers
Trees were heavy with pink and white blossoms
The fog lay across the bay where Hades lived
It had not come over the bridge
My mother and I went to a café full of lovely people
We ordered brightly colored Italian sodas
and French pastries
Then we went shopping
The store windows were full of ballerinas
and brides in tulle

My mother bought me a white lace vintage dress
with a full skirt
and pale pink leather boots with sharp heels

We went to the art museum
and looked at the visiting exhibit—
boxes full of weird things
china dolls' heads and hands
tree branches hung with crystal eyeballs
shattered pocket mirrors, a dead bird with one wing
paintings of goddesses that looked like men in drag

We sat beside a fountain and petted a golden retriever pup
Art students had set up their easels to work on the plaza
A clown was juggling
There was a skateboarding couple with dreadlocks
There was a man in a white shirt
with the sleeves rolled up, showing off
his brown forearms
He was reading a poetry book
and he smiled at us—bright teeth—
a toss of brown curls like a god in a painting

It was as if my mother had planned the whole thing
to show me what she could give me

That night my mother wanted to meet Hades
I told her no
We could go out together instead

The movie we saw
followed the lives of a group of children
Every seven years
the filmmaker made a documentary about them
The same children who had seemed so charming
and full of promise
changed
grew fat, sad, strange
I wondered how we keep from spoiling the angels
who come to us
I thought of the men I had known
what they must have been like when they were born
So gentle and small
I wondered if I could ever have children
knowing how I might damage them

Afterward my mother and I ate miso soup
and nightshade vegetable tempura
in a restaurant decorated with purple irises
She told me she still wanted to meet Hades

These mothers, they can be persistent

"It's really not that serious," I said
"I want you to know I don't blame you"
said my mother
"I blame your father
And my father for setting such a bad example"
My mother's father had swallowed her whole
and vomited her back up
My father had become a bull
a swan
a cloud
a shower
of gold
so that he could have sex with other women
It made sense that I would choose Hades
Who else would I choose?

I slept next to my mother
in the smooth, warm bed in the pretty hotel
The sheets smelled of bleach and chocolate
The city twinkled and murmured below us
I slept better than I had in years
But in the morning, over croissants and coffee
my mother asked me again

She said, "I have a small whitewashed house in the
countryside, not far from the sea. I bought it with the
money from the jewels your father gave me. I have
flowers instead of diamonds—they're not doing so well
right now, but you should have seen them! What they
can be! There is a wonderful college; you could go
there. We could drink wine and eat ravioli in the plaza
in the evenings. You should see the art! The men! The
light is rose gold at dawn, like blown glass in the
morning, like watermelon when the sun sets on the
city." She said, "I'm leaving today, I want you to come
with me"

But why should I leave?

My mother had left me
a long time ago
All I knew about her, really
came from the movies I had seen her in
the articles I had read
the smell of her clothes
She had abandoned me to her own hell god, my father
Now she was back, trying to take me away from mine
Why should I leave you?
"I'm not ready," I told her. "I am still with him"
"I want you back"
"But you left me. How can I trust you?"

There were tears in my mother's eyes
but she knew I was right
She left that afternoon
And I went back to hell that night

Whenever I felt pain I imagined that I was one step closer
to finding my lover again
I had completed the tasks of patience
self-denial and self-punishment

earned him this way
But what had I really done?
Given up a demigod of poetry
let myself be fucked by hell himself
Were those things enough?

Still, I told myself, I will keep trying

Until I am too old to want to be immortal

I dropped out of school and stayed with Hades
Every day was the same
I would wake late in the morning and make his coffee
After his shower I would help him to dress
combing his hair, choosing his rings
making sure his black leather pants fit smoothly
buckling his belt
helping him with his boots
When he left to make his rounds
I would do the marketing—
Chinatown for spices and dead chickens
Little Italy for fresh pasta and strings of sausages

The Lebanese market for rosewater and lamb
I spent the rest of the day cleaning Hades's house
polishing the black floors, dusting the artifacts
scrubbing the toilet
and cooking his evening meal
Before Hades came home I made sure I had bathed
put on makeup and a beautiful
dress
We ate together and drank red wine
at either end of the long table
We rarely spoke anymore
After dinner Hades left again
Sometimes he took me with him
to an opening of a club or to hear a new band
I held his hand and was very quiet
Usually I wore a dark lace veil over my face
When we returned home
the sky had turned pale with fog like a bride
Sometimes Hades grabbed me
in the large black bed
and sometimes he fell asleep
without touching me, his face to the wall

This went on for six months
I cannot say I was unhappy
I kept thinking that I was paying some important price
My dreams were full of dark treasures
china dolls' heads and hands, shattered pocket mirrors
a dead bird with one wing

I collected them to my breast
gathering my strength

After a while, I packed my things
and took an airplane to stay with my mother

Demeter lived in a whitewashed cottage
in the green hills above the sea
Every day was the same
I woke at dawn and bathed
helped my mother prepare breakfast—
muesli and fruit and cream
Then we went out into the garden and planted
pulled weeds and watered until the leaves
were emeralds

We went into the village
with cobblestone-paved streets
and bought fresh eggs and opalescent milk
Sometimes we went down to the beach
and swam in the sapphire water
We basked in the sun in giant hats
In the evenings we put on lipstick
and flowered gauze dresses we had made
and went to sit in the cafés
We ate pasta and drank wine
and watched each other glow in the candlelight
Men emerged from their marble prisons
So many speaking statues, perfect stone beauties
but we never went home with them
In the morning we gathered blossoms
that had bloomed overnight
This was the life my mother had bought
with the devil's jewels

I cannot say I was unhappy
But sometimes I would wake at night
in my mother's bed
and the smell of flowers through the window

made me wheeze, gulping for breath

Love, he was not there

Every six months I returned to Hades
Then to Demeter's garden
Back and forth between them aimlessly
I belonged to them
And there was something peaceful about that

So, finally
still seeking some kind of punishment
I went back to the city where my father lived

It is always possible to exchange
one hell god for another

Psyche as a Dress

I HADN'T SEEN MY FATHER'S GIRLFRIEND FOR SO LONG
I didn't recognize her at first
She was sitting in the front of her shop
fingering her dresses
as if she were touching flesh

There were some gardenias floating in bowls
It was a terribly hot day
and the air conditioner was broken
But Aphrodite never breaks a sweat
Cool as white flowers in a case of glass

I looked around the store

at all the things Aphrodite had made
There were dresses of petals
jackets of butterfly wings
or bird feathers
cloaks of leaves
coats of spiderwebs

Aphrodite and I spoke awhile
I told her that I was looking for work
and she asked about school, why I had left
I talked about Hades
It was hard to resist
confessing to a wide-eyed mother figure
She wasn't disturbed by what I said
I think she even smiled a little
Maybe just appreciating
a good story

"You could work for me," said Aphrodite
"You are one of my girls already"
I was still shivering a little
from the smile I thought I'd seen

a glimmer on her lips
like a trace of saliva
But I said yes anyway
That was how I began

I worked at the shop six days a week
I never even took a break
just wolfed down a sandwich in between customers
hiding the greasy paper under the counter
wiping mustard off my fingers
as I jumped up to help people

With the money I made
I was able to move out of my father's house
He hardly noticed
Since I had stopped performing in his films
I just wasn't useful

I rented a tiny one-room guest cottage
nestled away in a canyon
You had to take a steep path up behind the main house
to my miniature door

Morning glory vines grew over the roof
There were amaryllis and blue iris in the garden
Tomato vines and sunflowers
Blue glass wind chimes and a path of tiny stepping-stones
Inside, everything was so small I was always stooped over
There was no closet
so I gave away most of my mother's devil-dresses
washed my lingerie in the garden birdbath
and ate outside off a doll's china tea set
and seashell bowls in a ring of tea lights
When I was uncomfortable
I pretended I was in a storybook

In the evenings after work I hiked through the hills
and picked wildflowers for my hair
Sometimes I went alone to the local pub
and had a beer in the dark
watching the boys play pool
Then I came home to my room
with the claw-foot tub and the single bed
decorated with lace and cloth blossoms
from the ninety-nine-cent store

In this cottage I thought I had escaped my hell god
Maybe I had just found his female counterpart

Some days the shop was full of customers
buying up everything
and then Aphrodite was happy
She took me out after work
and ordered sushi and beers
She promised me a life of glamour, travel
wonderful dresses, any men we wanted

I got drunk and said I didn't want any man except one
"Who is that?" she asked, smiling wickedly
I told her about the god who had once come to my bed
The one I thought was a monster
"Oh, Psyche!" she said
"Is beauty monstrous?
What does that say about me?"
Some days no one came into the shop
and Aphrodite called every hour
to see if I had made a sale
her voice more and more frantic

Finally, she stormed in the door—
a whirlwind of red roses—
and demanded that I clean

I got down on my knees
and scrubbed the floor in my white clothes
while a few customers strayed in
stepping over me in their high-heeled shoes
I dusted the shelves in the back of the store
until I was caked with filth
I sorted through boxes of tiny beads and baubles
blue glass stars, abalone fish, quartz roses
jade teardrops, crystal moons
Aphrodite insisted that I organize them perfectly
without a single mistake
"Look at you!" Aphrodite shrieked
"There on the floor covered in dirt
How do you expect any man to want you
let alone that one?"
She put on a dress made of eucalyptus bark
snakeskin and rabbit fur and went off
to dance at a wedding

While she was gone the ants
crawled in from outside and helped me sort the beads
into their own little boxes
Aphrodite came back at midnight, drunk
"Slave," she said
"Witch"

She turned me into a moth
and shredded my wings to make dresses
But then she needed someone to work for her
so she changed me back
My hair was a little thinner after that
but otherwise I felt all right
She made me into a red rosebush
and plucked all the flowers for her dresses
While she worked she said
"Once I was in love like you
I pricked my finger on a thorn
when I ran to help him
My blood made the white rose red
so pretty
but what's the point?

He died anyway"

When she changed me back
my lips and nipples were paler than before
I guess I am lucky
Some girls never return to their original form

In this town there are a lot of dangerous types
I brought Aphrodite wool from the vicious golden sheep
to make her sweaters
I brought her drinking water
from a pool
guarded by dragons
I even went back to the underworld
to find the beauty cream to keep her young
Hades had a new girlfriend, who manufactured it
She was very sweet, actually
She reminded me of myself when I lived with him
wearing a veil, quiet, insecure
except she had a thriving business
called Deadly Beauty
On my way home to Aphrodite

I stayed at a motel on the coast
There were sea lions on the rocks
coughing their warnings
In the darkness of my room
I opened the jar and touched my little finger
to the pearly surface
patted it on my cheek

I was working at the shop when I got the call
My mother was dead

Before I dropped the phone
I saw the large black butterfly
beating its wings against the window
That was how I fell into an enchanted sleep
Why hadn't I decided to stay with her?
What would have been so bad about that life?
The gardens and the sea and the cafés
Was it only that I was afraid
what others might have thought?
Or had I sacrificed her to my lost lover
as I had sacrificed everything

He was still gone
And I had lost Demeter

I had chosen Aphrodite instead

I walked through my life in this strange trance
My eyes were glazed and my mouth was sealed
I worked at the shop all day and played pool at night
because it seemed like a good pastime
for a zombie in a dress
Even Aphrodite acted concerned
One day she came into the shop and handed me a book
"Read this," she said
It was so like my life
that I wondered if the author knew me

There was no photo
But it said where he lived
In my trance I wrote to him
Sent it to the publisher, never expecting a reply
I said that his book was just like my life
and that I would be in his city

Aphrodite was sending me there
to prepare for a trade show

A few weeks later a letter came

We met in the lobby of the hotel where I was staying
It was a small, romantic place with thick Persian carpets
striped satin chairs
marble and brass counters
flowers everywhere

I sleepwalked down the stairs
wearing Aphrodite's white peony dress
Love was waiting in the shadows
I had found him again

He stepped into a circle of lamplight
and it did not burn him

"I should have known it was you," I said

"You did," said Eros

"I wrote it so you could find me"

We stepped into the evening with hardly a word
It was summer and the sweat popped out on my skin
before I could take a step
The city was deserted this time of year
As I remember, there was no one on the streets
Eros and I walked along, speaking softly
He towered over me
even in my high heels I barely reached his armpit
A summer rain began to fall
misting my hair with a veil of drops
Eros took off his light tweed
jacket and draped it gently over me
His body was very thin but his shoulders were broad

We came to a small restaurant covered
inside and out
with broken bits—teacups, plates, figurines, glass
I wondered who had smashed the mirrors
not fearing bad luck

Eros and I sat across from each other drinking
white wine and eating
grilled salmon, couscous and salad
I couldn't remember having taste buds before
We were the only people there
The food just came to us by itself

"How did you write that book?" I asked him
"It's exactly my life. Have you been following me?"

Eros grinned a crooked smile
It was the first time I had really looked into his face
His head was shaved, laugh lines around his eyes
a nose with a bump, as if it had been broken
He had changed

"Maybe a part of you has been following me, my Soul"

Eros walked me back to my hotel
We shook hands in the lobby
No one was there
I could hear the rain on the glass

I didn't let go of his hand
Instead, I led him up the stairs to my room
He hesitated at the doorway, standing in the dim hallway
There were green cabbage roses on the carpet
faded gold and green striped wallpaper
A cart with some leftover baguettes and mineral water
stood outside someone's door
but no one was there
The only sound was the ice machine down the hall
The city so strangely quiet
Everyone was away, where it was cool and dry
The rain had stopped
"I'm sorry," I said, letting his hand drop
"No, it's not you"
"I shouldn't have assumed anything after so long"
"It's not you . . . I just . . . it's been a hard time"
I nodded and stood on tiptoe to kiss
his cheek without touching him
He steadied me with his hands
They were huge and bony
Most men's hands
are not bigger than mine

"Do you want to come in and talk?"
I turned on the lamp
He sat in the large cream damask chair by the window
The lights from the city shone in, fuzzy with the rain
I sat on the bed

"I would like to stay with you tonight," Eros said
"Just tonight
Then I have to leave"

I could feel my throat closing with tears

But what is real?
Maybe Eros and I stayed a month
a year
Who is to say?
Maybe we are still there now

When our lips touched
our clothes fell away
dissolving from our bodies
the white peony dress scattered its petals on the carpet

underwear disintegrating like cobwebs
Eros lifted me onto his hips
and I wrapped my legs around him as he fell
back into the cream damask chair
we kept falling as if through shifting
clouds
I could feel him inside of me
and that is how I awoke from the sleep of deadly beauty

After, we bathed in a tub that became the sea
with liquid topaz water and a beach of pulverized pearls
and we swam there and made love again

Then we ordered room service at midnight
ate omelets and grapes and bread in our bed
and the bed became an island
—covered with aphrodisiac flowers—
where we slept until late in the morning

Every day
I put on one of the dresses from Aphrodite's sample rack
And we ordered books and films and food

brought to the room
We lay in bed
reading and eating and memorizing each other's bodies
We wrote a play together based on his book
In the evenings we danced on the rose-covered carpet—
our ballroom
It went on like this for a day
a month
a year
I still don't know

I know only
that when Eros finally left I had his child inside of me

That was what made it possible for me to release him
even after the sacrifices I had made
even after waiting for so long

Do you want to know the name of the child
of Love and the Soul?
This is her name:
Her name is Joy

Eros

THE HOUSE WAS BUILT ON THE SIDE OF THE HILL, so it seemed perpetually to be sliding off. It was mostly glass so that one could see wooded hills and smoggy skies from almost every room. Eros's mother had decorated the house all in purple. There were purple velvet couches and chairs with purple silk beaded pillows, purple Persian carpets, giant purple candles and huge natural amethysts reflecting the light that poured through the windows. There was a terraced garden that Eros had planted with banks and banks of lavender, hyacinth, pansies and hydrangea—with pennies buried at their roots to make them the right color—and little fountains and statues of Eros's naked mother hidden among the foliage.

Eros was not unhappy. But as he grew older his mother began to suffocate him with her love. She couldn't help it. She had never loved anyone as much as herself before. No one had seemed perfect enough. He was perfect. But he felt as if he couldn't breathe. People acted strangely around him. They saw his face, smelled his skin and hair or touched his hand and something happened to them. It was as if all their senses were coming to life. It was too much for Eros sometimes. All that wanting.

He read the myths and learned that the god of love is not only the son of love and beauty but the son of chaos.

Eros felt empty, as if he had no soul. So he went looking for her.

He didn't have to go far. It was his mother who led him to her.

"My boyfriend's daughter goes to your school," she said. "She's featured in every single damn film. You should introduce yourself."

Psyche was the long-legged girl who kept her head bent as if to hide her face with her black hair. She always seemed so sad. He tried to talk to her but she wouldn't look at him. She hurried past in her odd dresses.

Eros could not help himself. He found out where she lived and he crawled in her window one night. He knew she was the part of him that was missing but he didn't know how to explain it to her. He thought that if she saw him she would send him away. Is beauty monstrous?

His mother said, "I heard that girl I told you about eats boys alive. She likes them really good-looking to feed her ego. Then she dumps them. You're so sensitive, sweetie. It's a beautiful quality. I just don't want you to get hurt."

When his soul finally lit the candle he felt betrayed, but he would have stayed anyway. It was she that sent him away. Afraid that she was not enough.

Eros packed his things and left. He traveled across the country. He shaved his head and ate only rice and vegetables until he lost so much weight that every bone showed. He practiced yoga and chanted. He went to museums and read books and saw films. He did not touch anyone. His skin broke out and he lay in the sun to burn away the red bumps. This left shadowy scars on his cheeks. He was called a freak more than once. Love is freakish to those who fear it. He was beaten up and his nose was broken. Love is a threat.

This was all right with Eros. Eros did not want to be a

god. He wanted to be a man. A writer would be nice, too.

Eros wrote about the girl who was his soul and in this way he felt his soul inside of him. He sent the book to his well-connected mother who sent it to her publisher friend. There was really only one reason Eros wanted the book to be published.

It was like writing a letter and putting it in a bottle and sending it out to sea.

Eros's mother had not told him about her new employee, the girl he had lost.

When he found her again he wanted to stay forever in that hotel room in the deserted city. He never wanted to leave her. But he was afraid that she would leave him. That she still felt she was not enough.

He might have tried, though.

Joy changes everything.

I AWAITED JOY IN OUR TINY COTTAGE

I made little films for my unborn daughter, little myths
Girls were transformed into flowers, trees and birds
but they always came back—
better singers, more fragrant, full of the earth's power
I stopped working for Aphrodite
I was afraid she might turn me into something
and not turn me back
There were other available slaves and witches to help her
and when you are about to become a mother
you just can't take as many chances

Even so, secretly, I wept for Eros
Part of me wished I had remained a flower
Passive, trembling in the sunshine
closing with the darkness
Waiting for some bee to pollinate me
It would have been easier than being a woman
much easier than being a mother

But I couldn't have stayed with Love
Although he had become a man he was still a god to me
And I?
I was a mere mortal
I was not a goddess

After I gave birth to Joy something changed, though
something I could not have predicted
There in the hospital room
I held her to my breast
and she took my nipple into her mouth
she looked up at me with long, still eyes
too large for her face
her fingers wrapped around mine
there was no one else in the world

Then I knew I could live without Love as a man
I had taken him inside me
and given him back to the world
in the form of a girl

I was hers—
my daughter's—
I was divine

Demeter

THEY SAY WE TURN INTO OUR MOTHERS

When my daughter became Persephone
I was Demeter

Just because I had loved Hades
doesn't mean I was prepared
when my child found her own hell god

He had one white eye and his nails and his teeth
were filed to points
Sometimes he wore plastic breasts on his bony chest
or a plastic phallus over leather pants

He wailed about carnage in a raspy voice

This is the one who took her from me

All I can think of is how, when she was a baby
she cried for me all the time
I was the only one she wanted
When I held her I didn't even need my hands
She clung to my neck with her arms
to my waist with her legs like a little animal
She slept in my armpit, her mouth on my nipple all night
It was the only way she would sleep
We woke in each other's sweat
She smelled like little white flowers
and baby soap and me—my milk

I had never been so important
to anyone
I felt as if I could make the world blossom
I had
I had made the world bloom with her

Then he came with his teeth
his nails painted black, his rubber clothes
his one eye behind a white lens like a blind man
He smelled of sulfur
He had a metallic gold limousine
and a driver with white gloves
This is the one who took my daughter away

I remember how we spent our days together
We had picnics with the dolls
on a red-and-white-checked cloth in the garden
ate off their china tea set
the tiny, bitter strawberries that grew in the clay pot
miniature carrots, tomatoes and sprigs of mint
drank homemade lemonade from seashells
We filled the birdbath with rose petals
and watched their reflection on the water
We painted our faces with rainbows
and wore giant heart-shaped rings
and wings
of gauze
We went to the library and read books

about baby animals
searching for their mothers
We sang songs of tiny stars, lambs, cakes
What was I thinking?
That this would be enough for her forever?

My mother had hoped the same thing
She had been wrong

My daughter screamed, "You'd say that about any man.
No one is good enough unless he's exactly like you."
She left the house

I want to believe that he put a spell on her
bit her
drugged her somehow
forcibly carried her away on his black motorcycle
But she went by herself
They broke glasses just to hear them shatter
and tore sheets with their hands
like animals with claws
They stayed up all night watching videos of him

dressed as a schoolgirl
His pieces
were about children killing each other with machine guns
about rape and explosions
bodies falling from burning buildings

People blamed him for inciting more of these things
but she said, "He is just a shy kid who was beaten up in
high school. A poet. He re-created himself to point out
the hypocrisy. He sees the world the way it is. You
pretend none of this exists. You live in a dream."

I wanted my dream
I wanted, more than anything
to make a dream and give it to her
to live in, always
But I didn't try to hide her from the world

She wasn't happy at school so I taught her at home.
I took her to foreign movies, gave her all kinds of
books. I let her wear lipstick and nail polish from the
health food store, although I told her she didn't need it.

I let her go to parties, even. I even let her go to that
performance of his. I wasn't too strict. I didn't cause
this, did I? I just wanted her to be happier than I was.

My own father swallowed me
and then vomited me back up
I blame him for what happened to her
If he had loved us she would never have gone away
with the god of hell
And I would not have needed my Hades
Or maybe it is my fault
I doubted myself
I let her real father go away twice

When she left I sat in the garden and lit a cigarette
smoked half of it and let it drop
thinking I could make a small pyre
a performance piece, almost
But the fire started to spread
After the fire department came
I felt guilty, of course
All those nice, strong men

who risked their lives to help people
Not clean up after some crazy, grieving mother
The ground was scarred and barren
She was gone

I thought, this is how I will repay life
for taking her from me
I will never grow another seedling
I will shrivel up in the darkness
and the flowers all die with me

Then one day I went to see
my daughter's Hades
He lived in a dark palace with iron gates and fierce dogs
A huge bald man let me in
He was smiling to himself, I knew
Smirking
Another mother trying to drag her stray child back home
He didn't think I was anyone to fear
I had not been a goddess before Persephone was born
Now I was a goddess enraged, protecting my child

A slender young man came down the staircase
He spoke softly and asked if I wanted a drink
I fingered the knife in my pocket
had imagined this moment so differently
Facing the hell god, slitting his throat
slaying him, bringing her home in my arms
All my fury at fathers and gods
would make me invincible

Instead I just stood there
looking at him with his soft unwashed hair
his stubbled chin and two blue eyes
like my daughter's eyes

He played the piano for me
a bunch of narcissus, white in a vase
The smell made me swoon, so I steadied myself
He sang of a mother and child
looked up at me, grinning, and said
"I could never put this on an album, though.
Reputations involved here"
She came down the stairs, in his shirt

Her legs so small and bare
When she saw me she looked
as if I were her hell

Then he reached out for her
took her in his arms
folded her up
I remembered
how light she once felt
and warm, perfect, safe

I thought
maybe any man who held her would be
like a hell god to me
maybe I can never
give her up
"I'm sorry," I said. "I'm sorry for coming here"
I let the knife fall from my fingers back into my pocket
I turned and left her there
I knew that I could never bring her back
The child I wanted to bring back with me was gone

It was winter
I took a bath in the claw-foot tub
and put on a white silk kimono with red poppies
I made corn, squash and garbanzo bean soup
on my hot plate
I watched the film I had rented
about a biker poet in a leather jacket
His wife went to the underworld
and he had to battle Death
who was not a man
but a pale woman with long black hair
I looked at myself in the tiny mirror on the door
I was no longer beautiful
I did not look like a former starlet
but I looked like an artist
a director of small, strange films
someone you could tell your story to in a bar
someone who had borne a daughter
(a perfect daughter)
someone who knew about planting
and pyromania

I looked like someone whose father had almost killed her
whose lovers had almost destroyed her
whose mother had tried to save her
had saved her as much as a mother can
whose daughter had saved her by being born
and then left her to save herself

One morning I was sitting in the garden
planning where I would plant the sweet peas
and the tomatoes when the weather changed
I heard someone coming up the hillside
My heart felt the way it did when she was a baby
and I had been away from her for a few hours
maybe she was just napping in the next room
but I hadn't seen her face or heard her voice for a while
and then she came in or called for me
and I would fly to her
needing her so much, missing her so much

I didn't try to touch her
She came and sat next to me on the singed wicker chair
"What happened?" I asked her. "Did he hurt you?"

"No. But I'm afraid he will leave me.

There are so many girls all the time."

"What makes you think he wants any of them?"

"I am not a goddess," she said. "You are."

This is what I told her

I have been young too

I have been Psyche, I have been Echo

I have been Eurydice

I have been Persephone, like you

I thought I was not a goddess

My mother was a goddess

Now I am Demeter, like my mother

Because of you

My Demeter tried to save me from Hades

That man you have is Eros too

I let my Eros, your father, leave

because I didn't think I was enough

But you must remember you are everything

We all are

Psyche means soul

What more is there than that?

Echo never stops her singing

Maybe it was Eurydice's choice to fade away

when Orpheus looked back

so she did not have to return with him

Persephone is a goddess of the bridge between

light and dark, day and night, death and life

Psyche

PSYCHE FINISHED HER FILM ABOUT A YOUNG
woman's quest. It starred her daughter, Joy, and her
daughter's boyfriend, the performance artist. Everyone
at the indie festivals loved it. They called it poetry. Psyche
thought, if I spend the rest of my life alone, it will be all
right. I have my art and I have my daughter back. What
more could a woman want? Aging is easier without having
to worry about a man.

One day Joy and her boyfriend took Psyche with them
to a dance. The room was filled with people flinging their
bodies around to live drums in front of an altar covered with
star-gazer lilies and beeswax candles. Psyche stood alone,
motionless in a pale blue sheer chiffon tunic dress covered

with sequins that reflected the light. She watched everyone—so young, so abandoned. In the eyes of all the men in the room she was no more visible than Echo to Narcissus. The music had no more power to stop her from getting older than Orpheus had the ability to bring Eury-dice back from the dead. She watched her child rolling on the floor, doing backbends and handstands, being lifted into the air.

"Come on, Mom," Joy said, taking her hand.

They danced together for a while and then Joy danced away but Psyche kept moving. It was easier than she had expected. Soon she forgot herself entirely. She forgot that she was probably the oldest woman in the room. She forgot that she hadn't danced in years. (Even then it had been mostly alone in her room with her mother's shadow.) After she had been in motion for a long time Psyche began to feel as if she were sixteen. She wanted to say to all the young women in the room, "When your mothers tell you to love and appreciate your body it isn't just to get you to shut up. They know that when you are old you are going to feel exactly the same way inside that you do now. We try on different dresses, different selves, but our souls are always the same—ongoing, full of light."

As she was thinking this, Psyche closed her eyes. A hand was at her waist. She didn't move but kept swaying to the music, feeling the pressure of the fingertips beneath her rib cage. She remembered how when she was Persephone, Hades had popped a rib out as if trying to get better access to her heart. What would he have done if he had actually held it in his hands? Her breath quickened and her legs lightened. All the blood moved to her chest. But her Hades had not come to claim her.

"Eros," she said.

When she opened her eyes, he was standing there. Had she conjured him with her dancing? He looked older now; his hair was close-shaven, nearly all gray. There was nothing about him that screamed "ancient power of the cosmos, love god, son of Aphrodite, son of Chaos." He was a man, getting older, her daughter's father. He was also her first lover, her secret, her storyteller. And he was a god, yes. But she was a goddess and a storyteller too. A soul in a new dress now.

My Mother, The Angel

MY FATHER CALLS HER THE ANGEL. I AM NEVER sure how to live up to such a mother. She is almost six feet tall. The planes of her face are like carved ivory. The long neck and smooth eyelids and high cheekbones of Nefertiti's famous bust. Strawberry hair cascading to her hips like Botticelli's Venus. Pretty impossible to compete with when you are just under five feet with faded brown hair and the face of an elf.

My mother can make flowers bloom with the slightest touch of her hand. Her garden burgeons— irises glitter as if embedded with silver, roses turn colors no one can match. Rose breeders come to find out her secrets but she only smiles mysteriously. They try to

analyze the clippings she gives them but it is useless—
the magic ingredient is her touch. Her birds of paradise are almost as tall as she is, her ranunculus look
like peonies, her fruit trees bear lemons that taste like
oranges and oranges the size of grapefruits. She can
grow star-gazer lilies whose pollen is as thick soft hot
pink powdered as expensive blush, and abundant peonies that people say only bloom in cooler climates. No
jasmine ever smelled so sweet, bathing the insides of
my nostrils and mouth with its twinkling white-and-
lavender fragrance. My mother wanders around the
garden in the hills of Hollywood putting her ear to the
cup of the petals or to the ground and, smiling mysteriously, proceeds to trim or water or fertilize each plant
according to its own personal instructions. Sometimes
I wake in the night and I swear I can hear the flowers
in the garden singing my mother's name through the
open window.

These things prove that my mother is not of this
world. Don't they?

If there is any doubt, it would be quelled by contact
with my mother's healing powers. When my father or I

have any kind of cold, headache or muscular pain, she touches us in such a way that the discomfort vanishes. A strange breath of rose and mint fills the room and then everything is better.

Unfortunately for me, my mother's healing powers do not extend to transforming a plain girl into a girl so beautiful that it would not have surprised anyone to learn that this girl's mother was a celestial being. She does not have potions to make one's limbs long and one's skin glow. She doesn't believe in coloring your hair or wearing makeup. Why should she? Her eyes seem naturally kohl-lined. Her hair naturally hennaed. She is not particularly into fashion. She only needs a few gauzy dresses that she makes herself and some bare Grecian sandals that lace up her long amber legs. High-priced fashion would be a waste on her; it would be extraneous. Therefore, she rarely took me shopping when I was growing up. She told me I was beautiful without lip gloss or mascara. But, then, angels see beneath the surface of things.

How else is my mother like one?

"Her cooking!" my father says. "Her cooking is the

cooking of a seraphim!"

She makes tamale pies, spinach lasagnas, Indian saffron curries, coconut and mint Thai noodles, grilled salmon tacos with mango salsa, persimmon bread puddings and lemon-raspberry pies, each one in minutes and without ever glancing at a recipe. She can never duplicate a dish twice since she doesn't write anything down and is always too excited about what she will make next, so my father and I are sometimes left pining for a reenactment of the almond enchiladas or the garlic-tomato tart. But we always have something else to look forward to. And my mother's food has almost narcotic effects—no matter how depressed or agitated we feel before dinner, we always relax afterwards into a dreamy stupor.

Also, my mother never gets angry. No matter what happens she always has a placid smile on her glowing Egyptian-artifact face. Sometimes I secretly wish that she would lose her temper and perhaps I even taunt her a little, to test her, but nothing works. My mother is unruffleable. She is like the da Vinci Madonna with a crescent moon hung on her mouth.

How wonderful, everyone thinks, to have a mother who is an angel, who never loses her temper, who can make birthday cakes even when it isn't your birthday—cakes so delectable as to be almost hallucinogenic—a mother who can take away the itch of insect bites with a whisk of cool fingers over your skin. People envy me my mother. A few children, encouraged by their parents, tried to befriend me just so they could come over and get clippings from my mother's garden and leftovers from her refrigerator. But no one realizes the difficulties of having an angel for a mother. It can make you feel rather insignificant, especially when boys ask you out just so they can catch a glimpse of her, waving good-bye, braless and in gauze, from the front porch. Especially when your father forgets to pick you up from school because he is out buying new lingerie for her again (even though she will forget to wear it) or when you ask him a question at dinner about your homework and he takes fifteen minutes to answer because he is gazing into the illuminated peony of her face.

My father found religion when he found my mother. He made the house a shrine, decorated with larger-than-life-size paintings and carvings of her. He lit candles and incense and sat and meditated every day. Unlike his mother, who died when he was eleven, my mother, who is years younger than he is, represents the nubile and healthy goddess who would never break his heart by leaving before he did. In this way she is eternal. She is his unprecedented blossom, his chocolate-cherry-swirl birthday cake, ultimately his angel.

I try to be grateful for my mother's graces and the love between my parents. It is a much better situation than most of what I have seen around me. Perhaps if I looked a little like my mother it wouldn't bother me at all. But as it is, I drift through her almost obscenely perennially lush garden, through her sacred kitchen, past the altar with the many images of her flickering in candlelight day and night, and wonder why just a little of the magic in the house could not settle on the bones and skin of my face or manifest through the tasks of my hands.

I am not angelic in the least. I smoke cigarettes and drink beer (my mother, after a brief stint with sugar in her youth, is utterly pure in terms of what she consumes). I can't cook or garden. I scald soups and plants die under my care. I have been known to fly into rages, especially before my period and especially if The Angel happens to placidly remind me that it is before my period. Occasionally, and mostly under pre-menstrual duress, I have stolen things—underwear, nail polish and lip gloss. The only things I know how to do well are shoplift, kiss and dance. None are particularly saintly virtues. And when I say dance, I'm not talking about ballet. My dancing is wild and unruly. I failed miserably at ballet although my mother had, of course, been coveted by the New York City Ballet when she was a child but had decided that she could not leave her family at that time because they needed her cooking and gardening and healing skills more than she needed the fame and fortune of the dance.

But ever since I was a little girl I captured neighborhood boys and made them sit in the basement and watch me. I dressed up in silk scarves and stolen underwear and played songs whose beat I could feel deep between my legs. While I danced a strange thing occured. I would have visions of what had happened to the boys. I saw boys being beaten, boys being shamed, boys crying, boys beating so they wouldn't cry. Sometimes the visions made me cry, too. When the dance was over I would kiss the boys. We rolled around the dusty musty basement floor in a tangle of sweat and music. I loved how they smelled and the taut smooth warmth of their bodies. They moaned with pleasure and whispered my name. Then they left and never came back. Although some of them would eye me with a mixture of longing and anxiety at school. My dancing would never have gotten me noticed by the New York City Ballet. But I did know how to move my hips, fondle my breasts, lick my lips, kick my legs, run my hands along my inner thighs, fall into the splits, writhe on the floor and remove wisps and slips of clothing while tears of passion slid down my face, so hot that it felt as if they were burning paths into my cheeks.

I wonder, is my mother angelic because she loves my father so much or does my father love my mother so much because she was always an angel? Was she born that way or was her angelic nature intensified by meeting him? Either way I'm not sure what that means as

far as I am concerned, in terms of ever finding anyone who would love me as much as my father loves my
mother, or whom I could love the way she loves him.

My mother told me once that I was a miracle.
Doctors said my father couldn't have children but my
mother never gave up. And then she had me. Am I the
miracle? Or is she?

When I was little, and still really just an appendage
of my mother, my father expressed his love to me as if I
really were one of her limbs. He carried me around like
a good-luck charm, showing me off to the people who
came to the gallery on La Cienega to buy his paintings.

"The little angel," he called me.

If I cried my father was usually the first one to
take me in his arms and comfort me. He felt like soft
caramel-colored corduroy and smelled like the cigarettes everyone smoked at his art openings and in the
teachers' lounge, and like turpentine. He called me
darling so frequently that I hardly knew I had another
name and sometimes forgot when I had to answer to it
at school. When I was big enough to hold a pencil he
sat and drew with me. He put my drawings up all over

the house, right beside his paintings. He even let me put paint on his canvases. He brought me with him to the art classes he taught at the university and gave me my own easel and paper and charcoal sticks. Then he gave me watercolors, acrylic paints and finally oils. I felt drunk on the smell of turpentine, the mystery of mixing colors on the palette. When I painted I felt proud and beautiful. I felt like my mother's daughter.

My father painted me almost as much as he painted my mother then. He painted me as a baby nursing at her breast, sleeping on her belly, peeking out from her backpack. As I got older he painted me sketching or reading with her. When I looked at the paintings later, I did not recognize myself. I looked just like a tiny version of my mother, her third breast, her second head, her miniature twin. At first I thought that I had changed a lot growing up, but when I saw photographs of myself—a little pale and pointed face, eyes always worried, peeking out from behind my mother's swirling gauzy body—I realized that this was not the case; my father was just painting me the way he wanted me to be.

As I grew older my father painted me less and less.

By the time I had breasts I had disappeared from his canvases altogether. For a while I could come into his studio dressed in exotic getups and I would dance for him, trying to see who he was. All I saw were visions of my father falling in love with my mother. Sometimes I came bearing my latest painting of a wild Beauty with a body made of lurid open flowers, hoping to get his attention, but he ignored me and my work. He even painted a piece called "Family Portrait" which depicted my mother—in her flower garden.

Before that summer these were the worst of my problems—an angel mother, a distracted and sometimes neglectful father. Then everything changed. Just when I needed my mother's powers most, they seemed to be failing. The doctors told my father he was dying.

My mother would not believe it. She began to cook.

She concocted potions full of odd Chinese roots. The burdock was long and black and hairy, the lotus roots were like pinwheels or flowers. The food of the immortals, my mother said. She soaked the seaweeds called wakame and kombu. She peeled the thin beige skins off gnarled hunks of ginger. She made brown rice and tofu and miso soup from a golden paste.

The house had to be assessed. My mother went around throwing out all the chemicals that might have toxic properties and putting crystals everywhere—in teacups and cereal bowls, in the bathtub, all over the windowsills and altars. First, she soaked the crystals in salt water in the sun to purify them. The house was a mess of rainbows. Rainbows poured across the walls. The crystals reminded me of tiny cities with cathedrals and towers. Sometimes I took the smaller ones and sucked on them like rock candy but they had a slightly bitter flavor. Then, guilty, I put them in a glass of salt water on the windowsill to make them pure again.

My mother bought books about healing and taught herself acupressure and massage. She bought a massage table and set it up in the bedroom. Delicate watery music spilled through the house. The rooms smelled of lavender and aloe and eucalyptus.

She wanted to heal him all by herself, with her roots and her hands and the songs I heard her singing to him at night, lullabies like the ones she once sang to me, filling up the house like rainbows from the crystals. But after a while my mother realized that it wasn't going to be enough. She drove him to the hospital for the treatments even though I know she hated them. She just washed her hair so it shone and put on a fresh dress and drove him there and sat with him and tried to smile at the doctors, who were entranced and, she hoped, inspired, by her beauty, and then she brought him home to her soups and her songs and her flowers. She made him a silk beret to hide his naked head. She cooked up strange-smelling herbs and gave him the tea to drink.

While my mother did these things all I could manage to do was go to clubs, get drunk, smoke cigarettes and sleep. In the burning heat of that summer, even after the sun went down, it hardly cooled. I wore the night like one of the vintage dresses I collected from thrift stores—a purple silk with rhinestone star buttons. The crickets shrieked.

I went to a nightclub in a Greek restaurant on the east end of Melrose with plaster reproductions of classical statues standing around the dance floor. There was

something creepy about the flat white spaces of their
eyes, I thought. I bought a rum and Coke with my fake
ID and drank it quickly (always thirsty) until my own
eyes felt like Christmas lights. My dance partners were
David and Venus de Milo. Although he was not the
most captivating conversationalist or dynamic dancer,
he was pleasing to look at. She was missing many body
parts but also quite lovely. At least I could pretend I had
companions.

I came home and went to bed realizing how long it
had been since I had been touched by anyone. I sucked
my arms to help myself fall asleep. The next day I had
to hide the bruises.

My mother was so busy caring for my father that
she didn't notice when I stopped eating. Even though I
was ravenous all the time I controlled my appetite most
of the day. Then, late at night, after a few drinks, when
the clubs closed, I went to all-night fast-food stands and
ate burritos in my car in big gulps, squishing the beans
and cheese out of the flour tortilla. My car smelled like
grease that summer, and the steering wheel shone from
my handprints. The next morning, disgusted, I wiped

and aired out my car and vowed not to eat all day. This lasted until about two A.M. Sometimes instead of burritos I ate powdered sugar donuts with colored sprinkles. The powdered sugar cut and stung my mouth. The sprinkles reminded me of the lights of the city, shiny and sugary and fake and promising and nothing. That summer tasted like a powdered sugar donut stinging my mouth.

I decided to make my hair a different color so I went to see Mars at his West Hollywood salon. Mars called himself that because he was obsessed with space; he was determined to find evidence of aliens. While he trimmed my hair, Mars rhapsodized about his journeys out to the desert. He discovered secret government testing sites where there was evidence of alien landings. These areas were completely off limits to the public but Mars managed to sneak under fences and across barricades with his camera. He showed me a series of blurry photographs of marks on the sand. His eyes flashed like spaceships and his mouth salivated when he spoke. I worried that he would cut my bangs unevenly.

This time it was much worse than that. Mars was

showing me a circular burn mark on his forearm. He said it was some kind of secret government tactic to keep him from visiting the alien sites. He was so excited about the mark, which he believed was more pure evidence to prove his theory, that he didn't concentrate on my hair. I should have come back another day but I was determined. I told Mars I wanted to look glamorous. What I really meant was, I wanted to look so beautiful that I could forget that my father was sick, beautiful enough that a boy would love me the way my father loved my mother, beautiful enough that when my parents looked at me they would forget their pain. I knew Mars couldn't do that but I thought he might be able to help a little.

Mars stopped ogling his burn mark, ran his fingers through his gold metallic hair, shook his head so that his many gold hoop earrings jangled and said, "I have just the thing." I was imagining shades of Marilyn and Jean Harlow to make me glow in the dark, but when Mars rinsed my hair I saw that it was not platinum at all but a frightening ghoulish shade of light green.

Did he mean to make me into a Martian? Mars insisted it was a mistake, that he had intended something else, but that he thought it looked fabulous, and, besides, if we tried to dye over it or bleach it out my hair might all break off, and maybe it was some kind of sign the aliens were projecting to him through me, to not give up and keep searching for them.

I was unable to speak. Mars didn't charge me and I left trying to force the tears back down my throat. My mother could have carried off the green hair. She would have looked like a sea goddess. But I was elfin and small and now, clownish. And ashamed, too, that something like this would make me cry.

Instead of going to a club I just drove. I drove the freeway past medieval castles and neon crosses and raggedy palm trees. I drove under bridges and past walls decorated with murals of runners, cops, movie stars, Betty Boop and one old lady with crystal-ball blue eyes and a crocheted quilt. When it was late enough they seemed alive, staring at me with their eyes and reaching out for me with their hands. I liked to drive fast to feel as if I was getting away. I played music as loud as possible and screamed the lyrics until my throat was sore.

When I got home, late, I crept into the kitchen to get something to eat. My mother was lying on the kitchen table, naked. Moonlight shone through the window illuminating her body and the crystals she had placed all over herself. She looked like a crystal statue from a tomb.

I stepped behind the door. After a while my mother removed the crystals from her breasts and abdomen, stood up and walked to her bedroom. I followed her and pressed my ear to the door.

I heard my mother say to my father, "Give it to me."

"What?" asked my father. He sounded as if he were talking in his sleep. "What, darling?"

"Give me the disease."

"No," he said. "No, I can't do that."

"I know what to do with it," she said. "I'm stronger than ever."

"No! I would never let you have it!" my father said. He was fully awake now.

"I would rather die than live without you," my mother whispered.

I had known my father felt this way. But not my

mother. My mother who had never once seemed afraid.

In their bedroom it was silent.

The next night I went out again. To a dank beery underground club near Hollywood Boulevard, filled with vampiric-looking boys and girls, some of whom wore tiny red-stained pointed caps on their incisors; at least I assumed they were caps. They drank the blackest red wine and crammed together in booths admiring their veins. There was one boy who had two lumps on his scalp; he was proudly showing them off to two girls and insisting they were horns. They looked more like the result of too much head banging to me. The boy jumped onstage and started to yell into the microphone about cancer. He looked right at me and his eyes and mouth shone like a jack-o'-lantern. He pointed his finger at me until I left.

I drove to the ocean. I liked to try to notice the exact moment when the air changed and I could smell the sea. Sometimes the smog was too much and I couldn't taste salt on my lips until I was almost right there. But this night was late enough and I got the smell way before. The ocean seemed to be calling me. I turned off the music and listened for it whispering. Maybe I would become a mermaid. I had the right hair. I would live in the swirling blue-green currents, doing exotic underwater dances for the fish, kissed by sea anemones, caressed by seaweed shawls. I would have a dolphin as a friend. He would have merry eyes and the thick sleeked flesh of a god. My fingernails would be tiny shells and my skin would be like jade with light shining through it. I would never have to come back up or go to clubs again. Boys would never send me away untouched and empty. I would never need cigarettes or vodka. It wouldn't matter that my mother could not keep my father from dying. Nothing would matter.

I was drinking a six-pack of beer, sitting on the sand at my favorite beach, a little private cove with black pebble sand where almost no one came even in the day, and I noticed a tiny light in lifeguard stand #9. It was a deserted stand that had been boarded up, with a big sign: NO LIFEGUARD ON DUTY. SWIM AT YOUR OWN RISK. But the light was unmistakable. And eerie in the misty darkness, like a dropped star, a scudding flame. Then

I saw someone sitting at the top of the stand. It was a skinny boy with lots of dark curly hair. That was all I could tell. He was slouched over, his elbows on his bent knees, and he was looking out at the dark, moon-iced, foam-sizzled waves intently, as if he could see whales or dolphins or magic islands or phantom ships.

Then I wanted to go into that water. I wanted it so badly that my mouth stung like salt and my skin tingled and I stood up and ran down to the shore. I wanted to go into the waves and find the thing the boy saw. I knew that it was better than what I was, than what my life was. It was something deep and far and soothing and dark and bright. It was without pain. It was like falling into the surging liquid herd of waves and becoming one of them and becoming nothing and everything at once.

I was a mermaid. I had green hair. I could go deeper and farther.

But I'd had too many beers. The water was so cold. And the waves were stronger than they seemed. Right away I knew it was too much. Part of me reached up like a hand trying to grasp for air but part of me sank in so easily like a fist, plunging deep deep in, flooded with sea until it was inside of me—a lover, in my lungs and in my heart and I was no longer the daughter of a dying man and an angel who could not save him but the daughter of the water.

The part of me that was the hand, though, it must have reached up. It must have seen the foam of the stars and the waves of the night sky and wanted that, too, and somehow now, the boy on the beach is running he is running toward me, having seen, not dolphins or whales or islands or treasure ships, but a drowning green-haired girl who may or may not want to be res-cued but he will swim to her and he will buoy her up in his arms and he will drag her to shore where her head is writhing with seaweed and her eyes are pummeled stones and in the black sea that follows, he will be her breath.

In the hospital I asked them how I got there and they told me a young man had brought me and then left. I knew who he was and I knew where I could find him.

I had decided not to tell my parents what had happened to me. Besides, what could they have done? They had other things to worry about; they'd hardly noticed that I'd been gone all night. I was fine, I told myself. I told myself I was lucky.

After a few days I went back to the beach to find the boy who had saved me. I saw the little candle burning in the lifeguard stand and I saw him sitting in the exact same position as the other night, staring out at the water. I stood looking up at him and he nodded his head, very slightly, but he didn't move. His curly hair was all in his face and he had on a pair of big funny glasses that had broken and been taped together and he was wearing a baggy T-shirt and faded shorts and he was barefoot.

"Thank you," I said.

He nodded again.

I told him my name was Echo.

And that was how I met him. My silent friend. My lifeguardian. The boy with the secrets on his back, the boy who never said what he was called.

I went to see him every night. We built sand castles

with arches and columns and moats and turrets and hidden passageways. I hated to lose the castles, but he nodded and seemed to say, *This is a part of it,* watching them demolished by the waves. We would sit for hours watching the waves break against the shore. Although he was silent I knew what he was thinking, about how he had dreamed of the singing and flashing and how it had seemed so far away and now here he was beside it on a night so warm we could have been naked, basking in moon. Sometimes he played me melodies on his battered mandolin or his old accordion. The music was sweet and sad like rain and trains and leaves in wind. I just liked to sit near him, watching his hair flop in his face as he strummed or squeezed. I liked to sit close enough that I could smell him. He smelled of sea and salt and blueberries. I wondered if he tasted that way. My mouth tasted of blueberries when I was with him. How did he taste?

He must have kissed me that one time, in his way, to save my life. But then he never touched me again.

At home I watched my mother sitting at my father's bedside, eternally radiant like a candle that had hypnotized him with its light. I wanted to be an angel for the boy on the beach.

I wore white gauzy clothes and spoke softly. I attempted to make sweet green corn tamales but they hardened and stuck to the corn husk so I brought him cheese and apples instead. I did not bring him flowers from my mother's garden—afraid he would want to know who grew such creatures—but I picked armfuls of wildflowers. I didn't smoke or drink in his presence. If I felt upset I kept it to myself. I didn't reveal anything about my mother, my father or my past of lonely kissing and desperate striptease. I thought these things would send him running like the boys who had appeared so mesmerized in the basement but ignored me in the school cafeteria.

My approach seemed to be working. He wrote songs for me on the mandolin and accordion; he built me palaces and at dawn, when I left, his eyes shone like the sun-sea-glimmered sand. But still he never touched me.

My longing was starting to ache so much I could hardly walk. I slept late and staggered around the house. I was always hungry but food didn't fill me so I mostly stopped eating. I was more and more thirsty the more I drank.

I wanted him. I felt it like an ocean filling every orifice, like the night I almost drowned. I wondered if I were my mother, if then he would touch me.

Sometimes I told myself I would have to stop seeing him. I was going away to school anyway, soon. I would find another boy there, one who wanted me. But every time I heard his music or saw his face or smelled his saltberry scent I knew that I could never stop wanting him. No matter how far away I went or who I met. Who was he?

I asked one night as we sat on the shore by our ruined sea castle watching the waves break under the foam-white moon. He looked at me with so much sadness that I wished I hadn't said it.

It was not until two nights before I moved away that he told me.

There were so many tears inside of me but I was holding them in and he was sitting staring at the ocean through the lenses of his big strange glasses and I could feel his tenderness as if I were in his arms. But I wasn't in his arms.

"My father is dying," I said.

He looked at me. I saw his eyes shining behind his glasses. *This is a part of it,* he was saying. *But I wish it wasn't. I wish I could make it not.*

"My mother is perfect," I said. "I've always wanted to be like her. But I'm not. I've always been jealous of her. But now I'm afraid all the things I'm jealous of are going to die when he does.

"I need you to touch me," I said.

He looked down at his hands. His whole body was shrouded in sadness. *I'm sorry,* he was saying.

"Who are you?" I asked. I was trying not to sob. I knew I would be leaving him so it really didn't matter but somehow I didn't want him to see me cry.

"Have I imagined you?" I asked. "If I'm imagining you then why can't I imagine you making love to me?"

He bent his head and pulled off his T-shirt. His body was lithe and brown, his shoulders slightly hunched. He turned his back to me and I saw what was hidden there, pressed damp and matted against his shoulder blades. The shabby soiled once-white feathers hung limply.

Then he huddled back down in the sand, hiding his

back against the lifeguard stand.

Another angel. A real one. An angel for a love. An angel who wouldn't touch me. What was I supposed to do? With my wildness. With my rages. With my desire and my tears.

I left him that night. When I got home the fragrance of the flowers almost suffocated me. My mother had filled the house—they stood in vases and floated in bowls. My mother was wearing a wreath of roses. She was massaging my father's feet with eucalyptus oil. He had the look of an opium eater—his jaw slack, his eyes feverish.

I went into my room and locked the door and blasted the music and got in bed and rubbed between my legs thinking of the boy on the beach. It went on and on until I was dry and sore. When I came it was in sobs.

The next night I went back to the sea dressed in 1950s silk travel scarves—Paris with the Eiffel tower and ladies in hats and pink poodles, Venice with bronze horses and gondoliers, New York in celestial blue and silver. I brought candles and lit the candles, all the candles, in a circle around the lifeguard stand and put a tape in my boom box. I came down that ramp with the sea lapping at my feet and the air like a scarf of warm silk and the stars like my tiara. And my angel was sitting there solemnly in the sand, sitting cross-legged like a buddha, with sand freckling his brown limbs and he watched me the way no boy had ever watched me before, with so much tenderness and also a tremendous sorrow, which was what my dances were about just as much, the sorrow of not being loved the way my womb, rocking emptily inside of me, insisted I be loved, the sorrow of never finding the thing I had been searching for.

What was the sorrow of this boy? As I danced the visions came. A boy crying under a bed in a dark room. A boy shivering from cold, dreaming of sun to burn the chill away. A wound on the inside of his thigh. A boy on a bus running away from home to live in a lifeguard stand by the sea, a boy who had pasted wings to his back as the only way he could escape the pain of who he had been before. A boy who could not touch because if he touched he would remember things he needed to forget, reopen wounds he needed to keep sealed. A boy who could be safe and untouched as long as he was an angel, an angel and not a boy.

Afterwards I came and lay beside him. My heart was like the waves.

He took off his glasses and I saw, clearly, for the first time, the bones of his face. "Your heart is beating so hard," he said into my hair.

His voice didn't startle me. It was as if I'd heard it all those other times he'd spoken silently.

"I was so scared," I said. "I was shaking."

"You are beautiful, Echo."

Then I said, "It doesn't matter if we never make love." I just needed him to see me, feel what I felt. I just needed to dance for him and lie like this by the sea, with our tiny blue ark for when the flood came.

And then I cried a flood of tears as if I really were a mermaid who had absorbed too much sea into herself. The tears spilled like a balm, like a potion, like a charm. In them swam a little girl whose father was dying without ever having seen her. In them swam a girl whose mother's magic—the thing the girl envied more than anything else in the world, the thing that had made her invisible, the most precious thing—might be dying too. In them swam a green-haired girl who had never been touched by the boy to whom she was so devoted that she would have lived with him forever in a shack by the sea or a ruined sand castle even if he never made love to her. My tears were for me, but they were also for him. They were to wash away the thing that had frightened him so much so long ago. The thing that had hurt him so deeply. The wound inside his thigh. My tears poured out of me and he drank them down his throat. He drank them in gulps deep into himself, swallowing sorrow.

"Someday," he said, "when we are ready, I will give you back your tears."

When I looked up he was gone. I thought of the wings. Were they false, were they real? They were beating inside of me.

Enchanted Hotel

EVA SPENT HER DAYS IN THE WOODS WITH HER father, Sy, picking berries that ripened at the sight of her, swimming in lakes where fish and birds gathered to watch her, and studying the patterns of the wings of the butterflies that chased her. Meanwhile, her mother, Bella, stayed in the white wood-frame house overgrown with roses, writing stories. Then Bella was offered a job in the studios so she and Sy brought Eva to Hollywood.

Now Bella sat in a tiny bungalow on a movie lot, writing scripts that were stolen by producers who attached their starlet-girlfriends' names to them. Sy attempted to sell homes in the style of pagodas, castles, villas and chalets to people who never seemed to buy them. And Eva was left to fend for herself.

The jade-green hotel where they lived looked like a fairy-tale palace. Eva sat by the pool talking to the palm trees. She told them stories of eastern trees that changed colors and lost leaves, and heard palm tales of kissing movie stars and drowning children. Eva believed the place was enchanted, not realizing that she was the enchantment. She picked oranges and avocados when she was hungry and she floated in the water all day until her ivory skin turned to gold and her hair grew even longer, down to her knees, and people staying at the hotel would stop speaking or choke on their drinks when they saw her floating or perched in a fruit tree with hibiscus flowers in her hair and powder-blue or pale-yellow parakeets on her shoulders. A famous movie director spotted her weaving a nest out of twigs, branches, feathers and dried flowers; she planned to put it up in a tree so she could sleep closer to the moon on the warm nights when the pool glowed like a blue ghost. He was sure she was some kind of supernatural being and that if he could capture her on film he would change the history of cinema. However, she wasn't interested in becoming a film star, afraid that it would take her away from her family and corrupt her healing powers, so she pretended to be deaf and mute whenever he was around. Eventually he gave up and she was left alone to swim, build her nest and care for her parents. She learned to cook at that time, experimenting first with mud-and-jacaranda blossom stew for her bisque dolls who ate it voraciously and began to develop an uncanny human glow in their blue glass eyes, and eventually gathering recipes and tips from the people at the hotel. An Indian businessman taught her about curries, the aphrodisiac properties of certain spices and how to make a mango-yogurt concoction that was refreshing on the most burning days when the palm trees seemed about ready to ignite from the Santa Ana winds sizzling through their fronds. A couple who had come from China to open a restaurant, familiarized her with dishes employing mysterious healing roots. And a handsome Italian with fistfuls of black curls, dangerous cheekbones and hopes of becoming a matinee idol gave her his mother's secret recipe for risotto that shone in the dark. At the hotel Eva also learned secrets of a southern Californian garden from the three-foot-tall gardener who had played a munchkin in *The Wizard of Oz* and who knew how to breed impossibly green and silver hydrangeas, about the poisonous and thoroughly Los Angelean beauty of belladonna and oleander, and the arias that roses most enjoyed hearing. The plants immediately took to Eva and the garden at the hotel began to grow so profusely that the head gardener had to hire three more men to keep it from overgrowing the building. In the same way, all the exotic pet birds from the houses in the hills flew away from home to live nearer to the little girl. The trees shook and flashed with them. Stray dogs and cats also became a problem. A silvery-taupe weimaraner with pale green human eyes and a limp; an emaciated, low-slung basset hound who tripped on his ears; a blind honey-blond retriever with a perpetual grin; and various assorted mongrels descended on the hotel, following Eva around in a procession, bringing her flowering branches and offering her rides on their backs. Cats came, too. They lolled at the foot of the trees where she slept, crawled in through her window and ate at her table when her parents were out. The dogs and cats grew fat, huge and glossy in Eva's presence and from her care. She groomed them, stroked them, played with them and made them a special diet of turkey, oats and fresh vegetables. The blind retriever regained sight in one eye and the weimaraner stopped limping. They were so beautiful and good-natured under her influence that everyone at the hotel began to gladly welcome them into their own rooms and many canine and feline lives were saved.

One day, sitting at the soda fountain in the hotel cafeteria, Eva saw a man with shining sunken eyes and beautiful hands watching her over his cup of coffee and sketching strange sad-eyed creatures on his napkin. He was much older than she and never spoke to her, but she knew that he was in love with her and that one day they would meet again and become as inseparable as identical twins who looked nothing alike and had been born many years apart.

Sol was tall and thin and wore tiny round spectacles and a threadbare dark suit. Rose was very small, with a broad pale face. They met at a German synagogue when they were teenagers and never looked at anyone else again. After they married, Sol and Rose lived in a stone building full of candles and books, with window boxes of herbs and tiny vegetables. Sol taught philosophy to boys in a poorly lit basement. Rose was a milliner. She made hats piled with doves, flowers, cherries, peacock feathers, cupids for the rich women of the city. They were said to have certain unusual properties, the hats—love spells, fertility charms, talismans of prosperity and protection. But they were not magical enough.

When he was eleven, Sol and Rose's boy was sent away from his home to live with his aunt and uncle in New York. Before he left, Rose gave him her wedding dress wrapped in pale blue tissue and a box of paints and told him that if he ever wanted to communicate with her he could do so through his art. The boy had not understood what this meant. When he learned what happened to his parents, he became a little old man. He began to walk stooped over and the grief tasted like ash in his mouth. When he tried to paint images of the exotic birds and fruits that his mother loved, he ended up with monsters howling in dark storms and ripping their own limbs from their sockets.

So the boy began a desperate search for a woman with flowers growing out of her head, birds on her shoulders and the ability to mend broken hearts with her creations. There was no sign of her for years. Then he realized that he wouldn't find her in Manhattan, a city of dark stone and soot and noise and burning cold winters where nature had to be imported and relegated to certain areas like a caged animal. He imagined she was living in a sun-blossomed paradise, a city of magicians, movie queens, love-struck clowns. So he took the empty box of paints his mother had given him and the wedding dress wrapped in pale blue tissue paper and left the brownstone apartment, where he lived in a perpetual silence with his aunt and uncle, and went to Los Angeles to find her. Sitting at a soda fountain in a hotel restaurant, he was shocked to see beside him a little girl with satined skin and a white dove perched on her garlands of rose-colored hair. She was sipping a root beer float in a state of bliss. He heard the fizz of soda and cream, smelled the caramel dark; her hair was waves of petals, her hands were carved ivory amulets, tiny enough that he could have worn them around his neck. He said a prayer to a God he had ceased to believe in. He vowed to wait for her, to never let himself love anyone else. But one day she was not at the counter sipping her float. She and the enchantment were gone from the hotel.

Years later the artist who called himself Caliban had an art opening in a gallery. The paintings were of monsters from the depths of hell, monsters with gaping mouths and huge bleeding hands. Sometimes Caliban set real bones and skulls into the thick smeary dark paint. Once he put an entire skeleton in. He called the skeleton Mister Bones. The paintings were huge and sold for lots of money but Caliban was miserable. He vowed he would start painting something beautiful. The trouble was, he never saw anything that he believed was truly beautiful. Until that night.

She was standing among the monsters and casting an eerie light onto the bleak canvases. In that light the monsters appeared to be transforming. They seemed to be getting smaller and weaker. Their mouths closed and their hands dropped sheepishly to their sides. No one wanted to purchase these watered-down versions of Caliban's earlier work. They left the gallery in droves until the only person left was a woman who resembled Nefertiti with blushing hair. Caliban approached her and said, "What have you done to the monsters?" The woman smiled and it was like a temple full of candles, like a garden full of white flowers, like the spread of wings. At that moment Caliban knew that she was the little girl at the soda fountain in the jade-green hotel and that from then on he would never paint or love anyone else.

Thorn

I LAY ON THE BED IN THE DARK, TOUCHING THE BONE basket of my ribs, the bone bird of my hips. Although I was wrapped in blankets I felt cold. The room I shared with Thorn was really a sunporch. All summer we had looked out at the fruit-heavy plum tree and the honey-suckle vines and felt the sun through the glass panes. But now it was autumn, and raining. The tree in the yard reminded me of Mister Bones.

My stomach made noises like a cat as I curled up under the blankets. I did not shut my eyes. I did not want to see what was there in my head—the naked body, all bones and whiteness, crouched in a marble box. I could not escape the voice that easily.

I will not eat cakes or cookies or food. I will be thin, thin, pure. I will be pure and empty. Weight dropping off. Ninety-nine . . . ninety-five . . . ninety-two . . . ninety. Just one more to eighty-nine. Where does it go? Where in the universe does it go?

That morning I had walked all the way to campus, across campus, up into the hills of Northside to the hospital, knowing it would burn off the apple I had eaten when I woke up. On the way I passed a group of homeless men and women spare-changing near People's Park. Among them was a beautiful young blond girl in tight jeans. She whirled around and her face was not a girl's at all—a toothless crone's collapsing into itself.

The psychiatrist asked, "Why are you starving yourself?" and I had known all the right answers. Escaping the responsibilities of growing up; having control over something at least; being beautiful, perfect like my mother, making my father love me. I smiled secretly to myself that I could know all this and still skip dinner, still jog five miles in the rain. I did not tell the psychiatrist about Thorn.

During the first months away from home I had wandered on the campus looking into the faces of the men, searching. They were sleeping on Shakespeare in the cathedral-like library, slurping coffee from huge cut-glass goblets at cafes; they were on running shoes, on wheels. None of them was the one I was looking for. Then at a party in a warehouse near the Oakland border, I had seen Thorn wearing a white cotton shirt and drinking gin. There was something about him that reminded me of my father when he was young. Thorn was doing magic tricks, making people's jewelry vanish. He pulled a tiny orange paper parasol from behind my ear and walked me to the dorm. The air smelled rich and sooty after the rain, like flowers could grow in it.

"You look like a poet," I said, when he told me what was in the notebook with the torn binding.

"It's all just this pretentious self-centered angst."

I said I bet it wasn't.

He said, "Besides, don't I look more like a magician?"

When he kissed me good-night and held me for a

moment I was surprised at how cool his skin felt, except for the heat in the hollow of his back. The memory of that heat stayed in my palms all night. When I touched myself in my dorm bed, I said his name out loud in the dark. I wanted to tell him that maybe he had already changed something.

A few nights later we went to a cafe in the city with sawdust floors and steamy windows. Thorn lit my cigarette and talked about the beats who used to hang out there, bopping berets, snapping fingers, guzzling wine.

A skinhead with a swastika tattoo walked by the window screaming and I felt my knuckles whiten around the edge of the table.

"I don't think violence is ever justified," Thorn said, pouring me more bright gold from the glass decanter.

I wanted to make the swastika bleed. But to Thorn I just said, "Never?"

He must have heard the tightness in my voice. He looked out across Broadway at the nipples of a neon sex goddess flashing on and off. "I know. Maybe."

He bit his lip. It was soft in contrast to his narrow aristocratic-looking face. I felt my thighs weaken, like the muscles were sponges soaking up wine.

That night in his tiny dorm bed, the heat I had discovered in his back pulsed through my whole body. I looked into his eyes and saw myself trapped in the irises.

After that, we were inseparable, always holding hands, always touching, bound together. Nothing else, no one else mattered. It was easier that way. Most weekends we took the BART to the city and pretended to be different people.

"What do you think of the way Vermeer used light?" I asked him. We were on the lawn beside the ornate terracotta dome, watching the swans and ducks gliding on the pool. I was playing the older woman, the artist with a gingerbread house full of charcoal drawings and flowering cactus plants that you had to water very gently by pouring drops just into the center of the spiny leaves. The frankincense and myrrh woman with the huge hoop earrings and turquoise rings from a New Mexican reservation and the lines carved around her eyes.

He squinted up at the straining muscular backs of the stone men supporting the dome. "You'll have to take me to some museums," he said. He was being the young man on the road, following the sun because gray weather made him suicidal, writing his poetry in his mind in diners and gas station men's rooms across the country. "But I did see a show of Hopper once. And I like his light. It was kind of lonely or something."

Or, "'The world's a mess, it's in my kiss,' like John and Exene say," he mumbled. We were in a leather store on Market Street being punks on acid with skunk-striped hair and steel-toed boots.

"Fuck yes. Let's go to Mexico, shave our heads, get drugs, wear beads and silver."

Once, alone on the train, late at night, he pretended to be a professor teaching me about Dickinson.

"Why do you think she loved death so much?"

"She loved life."

"But she wrote about riding in his carriage, sleeping with him."

"That's because she loved life too much," I said.

He reached up behind me, so quiet, and slipped his hands inside my shirt.

If Death is your father, you don't ever have to worry

about what part of his body the disease will strike next. If Death is your lover, you don't have to be afraid that he will ever leave you.

We were opium-den dragon chasers in Chinatown, Santeria priests in the Mission, gay men in the Castro, tie-dyed acidhead sandalwood-scented runaways on Haight Street. No matter what roles we played at the end of the night we merged in the bed. We even began to look alike.

"If I were a boy I'd be you."

"You'd be wilder."

I chopped my hair shorter again and wore his shirts. The shirts smelled musky, like sweat and like peppermint soap, like him or like us, I wasn't sure. Sometimes I put eyeliner on him and he was prettier than I was. Men in the Castro stared. Leather-chapped chaps and pale pierced boys.

Then I gained a few pounds from all the Sunday croissants that soaked buttery stains through the napkins, the Kahlua and milks, and from the birth control pills I had started to take. I dug my nails into unfamiliar flesh—the breasts, the hips. It was like they belonged to another girl. Thorn stayed so thin.

Once, near the end of the semester, I broke an empty
gin bottle—threw it to the floor and felt it shatter as if
it were a part of me, as if the bones in my wrist were
glass splintering. Thorn held me, hunching his shoulders to shield me, and I choked on my tears, squeez-
ing my belly, disgusted by the extra pounds that had
lumped themselves there.

In June, Thorn and I moved into the blue wood-
frame house full of students. We had to step over two
sleeping bodies to get to our glass room. Through
the walls we heard moans of love and people screaming at each other. The kitchen floor was always sticky
and the refrigerator overflowed with fattening foods; I
had dreams of chocolate cakes ascending the stairs and
smothering me in my sleep.

But the room was pure, it was cool, it was glass. We
filled it with the thin, hard things we had collected—
old Iggy Pop and Velvet Underground albums,
narrow volumes of Emily Dickinson's poetry, posters of Picasso's blue, bony, ravaged, absinthe-poisoned
saltimbanques, a wine bottle holding dried flowers.

The room smelled of new paint and the sweet straw mat on the floor.

I went off the pill and started to lose weight. While Thorn was at work at a cafe I lay in the garden sun, letting the warmth burn into me. I waited for Thorn to come home; there was no one else I thought of spending time with. On weekends we took drives along the coast, jogged in the hills, went to museums and flea markets where I bought deteriorating silk slip dresses from the forties. We read poetry in cafes, took photographs of each other. There was a slowness about us. We didn't stay up late anymore, sawdust whispers over wine, beat-love poetry all night.

By the end of the summer something was changing. Thorn seemed preoccupied, distant, staring into his coffee or his book. After we made love we slept apart. The single futon seemed too small for the first time. I would turn away and fill my lungs with air. Thorn ground his teeth in his sleep.

When we went out I noticed all the women—wishing I was tall like that, golden like that. African women rippling beads, braids, sarongs and silver; shiny

Asian girls with colty legs; women with flows of fruit-colored hair; there were broad cheekbones, tiny sculpted noses, gemstone eyes. A parade of the pieces of women. My own eyes that were not gemstones, were not tourmaline or jade or sapphire, darted from the women to Thorn. I thought of my mother who was more beautiful than all of them.

I hadn't gotten my period for two months so I went to the doctor.

"You're not pregnant," the doctor said, and I didn't feel relieved or sad, just emptier. "Have you been eating?"

I told Thorn that night, "I think I'm sick."

He didn't say anything, just looked at me, glazed. I wanted him to call me darling. Tell me it would be okay. We'll take care of it. It was what my father might have said when I was a little girl. I wanted Thorn to take me out for dinner and order brown rice and vegetables and white wine.

That night we lay in the darkness in the bed and I shivered, my stomach growled.

"Thorn?"

He sighed. "What's wrong?"

"I can't sleep. I feel weak."

"You should eat something then."

He turned over. His back was a fortress of bone. I curled up, my head under the covers, wondering what it was I wanted from him.

I heard the grind of molars next to me in the bed.

Thorn was hesitating outside of our door. I heard him rustling. Then he came in and flicked on the light. It burned my eyes like a chemical. The rain had darkened his hair, pressed it against his skull. He held up his empty hands, then reached behind and brought out a bouquet of roses.

I hated the roses. I couldn't help it. I hated the pink wet trick roses he was holding. They reminded me of the morning I woke up to a bed covered in roses he had stolen from the neighborhood and then clipped to remove the thorns. The way we had made love, crushing petals until the whole steamed-glass room smelled of pollen and sex. They reminded me of his wounded-looking mouth as he read his poems.

Thorn handed me the roses and took off his tweed jacket. The water had gone through to his shirt so that it stuck to his thin shoulders and chest. He was the same white as his shirt.

"Thank you, Thorn," I said in a voice that sounded too controlled, too cold. I didn't mean it to. I put the roses down beside me, trying to keep in mind exactly what I was going to tell him.

"I have to talk to you," I said.

Thorn sat on the narrow bed with me. I could smell the rain that had soaked into him, starring his eyelashes. I tried not to think of how I kissed those eyelids, how the eyelids trembled when he came.

"I'm going home. I dropped out of school today. My parents are coming to get me tomorrow. I'm sorry I didn't tell you first but I have to get out of here. It's not you. I need to be home now."

I had not told the psychiatrist about Thorn. Or about my father.

Nothing my mother could do had helped. Nothing the doctors could do. They had treated him and now there was more.

I had tried not to let my father know about the cat in my stomach, the way my skin bruised at a touch, the metallic ache of my teeth. How the only thing that made me feel calm was seeing the scale register less and less weight. I didn't say that all I wanted was to move back home. Maybe I could help my mother take care of him. If he let me take care of him it might be as if he were taking care of me.

It came out that night on the phone. I started crying to my mother and he took the phone away and made me tell him. The psychiatrist. The lost pounds. The cat, the bones, the metal, the box. And then I heard him speak, in a voice I had almost forgotten.

He said, "Stop saying you're sorry, darling."

He had not called me that in years. He was going to get in the car, even though it hurt him to sit for too long, I knew that, and drive up to bring me home. He had waited until I stopped crying, stopped apologizing, and said, "There's only one condition. We're going to stop for a Foster's Freeze on the way. And you know how I hate eating dessert alone."

I wondered what had happened. Had someone flown down and whispered something into his ear?

One weekend soon after we'd met, Thorn and I had gone to stay in the house where he had grown up. Thorn's father was away on business. The house was an old wood-and-stone two story with a plot of wildflowers in front.

"My mother used to call it the meadow," Thorn said.

Inside the house was icy cold—so that our breath hung on the air—and dusty. "My dad's not a great housekeeper," Thorn said. We built a fire in the shivery living room and ate our pasta in front of it. Then we climbed the creaking cold stairs to the bedroom with watercolors of wildflowers on the walls, where Thorn's parents used to sleep, and where no one slept now.

"He stays downstairs in my room."

I started crying while Thorn was still inside me. I had wanted to ask him if he could feel the crying in himself, then.

"My dad has cancer." It was the first time I'd said it out loud.

And he had just held me, not saying anything, until I fell asleep.

The next night I danced for him in his father's house, removing my clothes, in spite of the cold. I wanted to give him something. I wanted to feel what he felt. I saw his mother, with bright eyes and dusky brown hair and full rosy cheeks, picking flowers from the meadow, painting them in watercolor, reading to her son, listening to him recite his poems. I saw his mother in a hospital bed, bones poking against her skin, while he tried to make her forget with silver rings and vanishing eggs.

After the dance, Thorn cried. And after that, neither of us spoke about my father or Thorn's mother.

Thorn bit his lower lip and turned his head away. He made a soft, nervous sound, almost like a laugh.

"Well, how do you feel? You never say anything anymore."

He breathed hard through his nose. His shoulders heaved. It was as if I could see the feelings locked between his scapulae and in his sternum. He looked at me, narrowing his eyes, breathing hard.

"I love you. I just have to leave. I'm a mess. And my dad is really sick." I was almost screaming. "Can't you say anything?"

"Just . . . let . . . me." He sounded strangled. There was a long silence of rain and breath. I started to sob into my hands. He watched the sobs shake my torso. My body felt like a child's, as small as when I was a child. The roses were lying next to me on the bed. Some of the rainwater had soaked into the quilt.

He did not turn around but stood facing the door, his hands forming fists, his shoulders stooped and rigid. I wanted him to hold me, to take care of me, to make the pain dissolve away. I knew that this wanting was part of what had ruined everything but I wanted it once more anyway. I rubbed my hands along the backs of my thighs to warm them. Then I crossed my arms on my chest and grasped my shoulders. They felt like the skulls of birds.

Finally, Thorn turned. I reached up and he took my hands, warming them in his own. Then he knelt and pressed my hands under his armpits. The heat of his body made my hands ache, then tingle.

We did not make love. We had not made love for at least a month. We had hardly touched for a week. But that night we slept close again, Thorn's hands solid heat on my abdomen.

I dreamed of my body all light and shadows in yards of sheer white lace. I was standing beside Thorn at the end of a corridor and he turned to me, lifting the veil that hid my face. He leaned to kiss me. I parted red lips of a skull revealing fanglike teeth.

"Mister Bones," I said, "pray tell, sir, which one of us is you?"

The next morning Thorn kissed my eyes. He made a small plastic dove ring appear out of thin air, unfurled my finger and slid it on. Then he left.

I lay on the bed waiting for my parents to come for me.

Smoke

WHEN, AT THREE, HE FIRST SAW *THE WIZARD of Oz* on TV, JJ fell in love with Glinda, the good witch. The tulle-haired, glitter-frosted queen with the little people hidden in her frothy cakelike skirt. For years, on every birthday cake he wished that he could find her.

Then, all he wished for was that his mother would get better.

His mother was pale fragrance and paper hands and then she was drowning among bouquets in the metallic hospital. When she died, he wondered what he had done.

His father the TV producer immediately began to collect starlets around the breakfast table, around the

TV-shaped pool. They petted JJ with their sharp red-lacquered nails and asked him where he had gotten those beautiful eyes.

They're hers, he wanted to say. And she is watching you. And she wants you to leave.

When he was thirteen, he felt as if he had poison in him. His skin broke out red and sore. He wore a cotton hat slouched over his eyes and got high in his room. The starlets ignored him. His father said, "When are you going to get yourself a gorgeous girl?" His sister Elaine bought him a tiny guitar with cowboy decals on it. JJ stood in front of his mirror and sang along with John Lennon and Elvis. He had Lennon's bone structure and Elvis's lips. He was thinking about his sister's friend, Wendy, whom he had seen in the backseat of the red 1965 Mustang convertible when Trina dropped Elaine off one night. She looked just like Glinda with her hair and her vintage dress covered with glitter stars. Maybe this was what John knew when he first saw Yoko, what Presley felt when he laid eyes upon Priscilla. Wendy was more lovely to JJ than any of the starlets. Than any of the star-gazer lilies his mother had loved. Than any of the stars in the cosmos. But he hardly ever got to hang around her; Elaine didn't bring friends home because of the starlets and he was too shy to ask.

Then, four years later, Elaine started Babylon with Trina, Jeff and Wendy. One night, she asked her brother to come to a rehearsal.

JJ was tiny but his hands and wrists were broad as if he should have kept growing. Marbly arms and narrow hips. Delicate features and the shadowy blue eyes of— what? Wendy thought—wounded, erotic, narcotic . . . the eyes of a beautiful dead woman.

He was what the band needed. His voice seemed to smolder in his chest before it came out his throat.

Smoke, they started to call him.

"The voices make love onstage," a critic said.

Offstage, Smoke came to Wendy's apartment with the tiled courtyard and the fountain of demonic-looking cherubim. She was in her densely embroidered antique kimono and lace lingerie, writing songs. She rolled joints expertly and they smoked on her bed with the satin curtains closed, the mirrored ball scattering rainbows and Bowie's voice. Then their bodies were the smoke and color and music. Their eyes were always damp with love now, and their flesh was soaked with the scent of fire and roses.

"Did J and Wendy always have the same face?" Elaine asked Jeff. "He's supposed to be *my* brother!"

Jeff, who always looked hungry, was even hungrier now. He just lit another cigarette. He wanted to set the flowers he had bought for Wendy—again, compulsively—afire.

Wendy made Smoke big vegetarian dinners and brought him Native American tobacco that he had to roll himself. "You'll have less that way," she said.

She felt like his mother sometimes, making him wear his coat when it was cold out, making him eat his dinner. He lay against her breasts with his eyes closed. She sang to him and he put his fingers at the hollow of her throat to hear the purring hum.

"Wendy-Glinda . . . I dreamed all these people were trying to make this bush grow and it wouldn't and then you start singing and these roses start. . . ."

She laughed and put her fingers into the cool of his hair. "What do you wish for?" she asked him.

"For us to be stars. For us to tour Europe and play the coolest clubs. I used to wish for you."

"See," she said. "It works."

He didn't mention his mother.

They dropped acid and saw the same full purple waves peeling back like the petals of a flesh flower. They took mushrooms in the mountains, washing them down with milk, and thought their brains had melted together, burned under the white mushroom moon. The hash made them giddy—he performed for her, doing an uncanny Edith Piaf that made her scream; then they ate chocolates and kissed for hours. They hated speed, which made their nerves ache. Cocaine was okay once in a while, bolting white bulbs of light through them and making them feel as if they sizzled with beauty, but Smoke got feverish sick once and they cut it out.

But it was the opium they dreamed of. "I keep having visions of dripping blue poppy fields," he said. They smoked it on Wendy's birthday and felt floating on, stung with, clouds of powdered sugar.

"Hansel and Gretel tasting all the candy," Smoke said with an ache in his voice.

"We can't do this too often, babe," she whispered later. "We can't be junkies or anything." But he just licked his papers and rolled a cigarette and gazed across the room to where the mannequin stood in her rhinestones and her orange satin Chinese cocktail dress.

They moved into a house downtown with Elaine and Trina who had finally consummated the love they'd shared since junior high. Jeff and his new girlfriend Suze moved in, too. They were the only white people in the neighborhood. The house was crumbling—pale paint peeling—but it was beautiful with its gingerbread carvings, like an overgrown dollhouse. They cleaned and hung up lace and strings of lights, glitter stars and the drawings they'd made.

In the smoggy violet of summer evenings they sat on the dilapidated porch playing guitar and singing. The children from the neighborhood came and hid behind the posts, peering out with dark eyes, peering at the whiteness—the flash of what looked like diamonds at

Wendy's and Suze's throats and wrists and in Smoke's ear, at their bleached hair. But it was the music that brought the children to sit on the porch or jump rope and finally sing along in thin voices.

Maybe it was being around all the children that did it, Wendy thought when her period didn't come.

Being around all the children and that night in the rain. They had eaten curry and samosas at a restaurant shaped like a camera with the front window a giant lens. It was raining when they left. Smoke sheltered her with his leather jacket. Because she was taller, especially in her heels, she had to bend over to fit under his arm. They ran along the sidewalk, laughing in the blue glaze of streetlights while the cars sliced through the rain.

"I'm so wet," Wendy gulped, shaking out her hair when they reached the house.

She remembered his voice like warm honey in his throat. "Are you?" He pulled her hair away from her face and slid his hand between her legs.

"How do you know she'll be a she?" he asked, when she told them she was pregnant with his girl.

"We're daughter-makers."

She had Smoke's eyes and fine features, Wendy's full lips and smooth skin. She was fragile with bluish shadows under her eyes.

"She's the most beautiful thing in the world but she looks like she'll break," Elaine whispered to Trina.

The doctor found something terribly wrong deep in her spine. When Wendy told Smoke, he lit a cigarette and started coughing—a hoarse aching sound that seemed as if it would never end.

Take my soul, take me instead. During the operation he got down on his knees and prayed that he could exchange his life for hers. He had never felt this way—even when his mother died—that he would have given up everything. He would have given up his songs and the way he saw his voice rippling through the bodies of the girls at the gigs, almost as if he were touching them, and he would have given up the lotus festivals of the drugs and the wizardry of kisses, and he would even have given up, he realized, the one he had thought he loved most. *I would give up my life with Wendy for Eden.*

His nose was bleeding, flowing in a red torrent that had the force of his fear.

The operation was a success. After it was over he fell asleep for an entire day and night. When he woke in the fluorescent haze of the hospital waiting room, he wondered, for a moment, if he were still alive. It was only a partial relief. He was always afraid the disease would return.

One night, sitting on the porch lit with votive candles wrapped in saints, he said to Wendy, "I feel like I poison what I touch." Eden started to cry suddenly, as if she had been slapped. Smoke ground the joint into the ashtray and stood up. Wendy could see Eden's hurting in the hunch of his shoulders and in his staring eyes. He left the house.

He moved out to a windowless basement apartment that was hardly big enough for his single futon. His skin looked chalky and his pupils seemed to be disappearing. The wanting that had been in his eyes and shoulders, in the veins in his arms and in his mouth when Wendy met him, had come back again. But she couldn't do anything about it now. She started to go out with men, mostly tall, dark, husky men who couldn't sing.

Girls wanted Smoke. Maybe they wanted him more; his small size brought out their maternal instincts and, now, so did his sorrow. Eden liked one of the girls right away. Her name was Echo. Eden showed Echo the cast on her wrist; told her how she'd broken it when she fell; made Echo draw a portrait of Sea Shell, the mermaid doll, on the cast. Eden put her lipstick on without a mirror; she put some on Echo. They danced together. This was the reason Smoke noticed her at all. It was as if Eden's beauty reflected onto her, making her other-wise matte surface glimmer slightly like the little girl's rose-frost lip gloss.

Eden said, "Someday you will love her," and it made Smoke feel as if she had looked into his eyes like crystal balls but he didn't want to believe her; she and Wendy were all that was in his eyes.

One night after a gig Echo asked if she could come home with him. She wasn't beautiful and he didn't love her so it seemed all right at first. They smoked pot and watched some TV. Then Echo put on "When Doves

Cry" and started dancing. She was a completely different person when she danced, lush and feral. She took off her shirt and ran her fingers over her breasts. When she looked at him there were tears in her eyes as if she knew the things that had happened to him. His mother. Wendy. Eden. He remembered what Eden had said about her. Echo came over and knelt between his broad knees and he let her kiss him. She smelled powdery and sweet and nice and her eyes were almost as sad as his but when he felt desire startle up in his heart and groin, for the first time in so long, he pulled away.

"I don't want to hurt anyone," he said as if his throat was sore.

And Echo gathered her things and ran barefoot out the door. He knew she was crying. And that he wanted to cry. But how can I take the risk? he told himself. It's not worth it.

Eden was his goddess. He would sacrifice everything for her to stay in the world. And one night with this girl wasn't even close to everything. Was it?

As Eden grew up, Wendy made her dresses out of sequin netting, painted flowers on her face and brought her to Hollywood parties and nightclubs where people took their pictures for the local alternative paper nightlife column.

Eden smiled like a woman, went up to some of the men, put her hand in theirs. She asked softly to be photographed. She asked, "Have you known me since I was a baby? Was I a pretty baby?" She shivered and shimmered. Her voice was breathless. Her eyes were more and more Smoke's eyes. Waiting eyes.

She told her own versions of fairy tales, about how the prince did not kiss the princess awake but made love to her to bring her back to life, about how the beast never changed into a prince but gave Beauty little beast children who gnawed savagely at her breasts. When they asked how she knew these things she ran off shrieking like a mad cricket. In the morning she woke Wendy's lovers by crouching on their chests—a pretty gargoyle—and insisting that they tell her their dreams in detail. They fell madly in love, bringing her candy necklaces, writing songs about her, painting her picture.

Rumors spread that she was sick. People looked at

Wendy differently, said, "How *are* you?" in a different way. "And how is Eden?" Whenever Eden fell, she broke bones in her wrists and ankles. Raphael the mural artist drew on her cast. Candyman the lead singer of Icon lifted her onstage beside him and she danced. She wore a little rhinestone tiara. She was a star already.

Smoke took Eden to the movies once in a while. Especially *Fantasia*, which was her favorite. She made pictures for him and covered him with kisses. The color on her lips was lipstick, smudged and pink as candy. He hardly let anyone touch him now but usually he didn't shrink away from her. They held hands and walked slow uneasy tiptoe steps as if they weren't sure about remaining on the earth, and their blue eyes seemed to look through to something, some garden, something. Eden never said, "Dad," or asked who her father was and Smoke had asked Wendy not to tell her.

"When is Smoke going to move over here?" was all that Eden said.

He was never going to. He was afraid that if he broke his vow to give up everything for her, that she would leave. Only those afternoons at the movies; he allowed himself that. But not Wendy. His Glinda. Paradise. Sacrifice.

They still had Babylon, though. Their new manager, Dean, a tall, dark, husky man with a goatee, had a party at his glass house in the hills to celebrate their record contract—champagne, sushi, coke. Wendy was kissing Dean on the deck. Eden was running around ripping long green strands of hair out of Sea Shell's head. The doll reminded Smoke of Echo. She had told him that her hair was that green once, mermaid green. He thought of calling her. Instead he snorted some white powder and threw a microphone against the glass wall. It was like the city shattering into all those little green and red and silver lights. Wendy left Eden with Elaine and Trina and she and Jeff drove Smoke to the hospital with his wounded hand wrapped in Wendy's white silk chiffon scarf. Blood had dripped onto Dean's white carpet. Eden squinted at the stain, as if trying to see it as something else—the shape of a heart.

When she got older, Eden performed with Babylon. She was a tiny Wendy singing in a whisper, her wrist in a cast. Wendy knew it was okay when they were all onstage together. They were a family then and they were one person. Eden was Smoke and Wendy and Eden, and she would grow up to be a child-woman holding the secret of their radiance and their music and their wishes and their love in her pale-milky fragile bones. The garden where no one ever gets old. She would grow up healed and healing because their love had made her, Smoke thought.

This was Smoke's only wish now.

Caliban's Gift

WHEN I LEFT MY HEAD WAS BUZZING like a staticky TV screen from no sleep, my body from desire. I had seen Smoke's story when I danced. I saw the fairy girl with her eyes just like his. The one who had taken my hand in the club, painted my lips as if she were bestowing a magical charm. I saw him on his knees in the hospital waiting room, blood gushing from his nose. His wish for her. *Take my soul, take me instead.* He loved her so much, enough to give up everything. I couldn't blame him; she was perfect, more perfect for her fragility, for the fact that she seemed about to leave this earth. I wondered for a moment, if I had gotten sick like that, what would my father have done . . . but you can't think that way.

I climbed up the stairs out of Smoke's apartment, ran barefoot over the dewy lawn, my shoes in my hand. I knew not to drop one. This wasn't anything Cinderella. I might never see him again, let alone expect a visit with a glass slipper. The sky was bleached out and the birds were strangely still. I wanted to stop for a bag of burning-sugar donuts, go home, take a bath and stroke myself to sleep.

The ambulance was parked in front of the house. I saw my mother shivering in a coat over her nightgown. She seemed much smaller, like a child who had not grown into the length of her hair. She said to meet her at the hospital and then she climbed in the ambulance and they shut the doors and drove away. The siren sounded weak, not urgent—hopeless.

I followed through the empty streets. There was a faint metallic light at the edge of the sky now. I thought, what if Smoke and I had made love, slept in, gone out for pancakes, walked in the hills, kissed in the wildflowers while the sun came up to bake the petals. I wouldn't have been here for hours.

My father was lying in the hospital bed and my mother was holding his hand, talking to him. His mouth was open and his eyes were closed. I didn't know if he was taking death in through his mouth and shutting out life with his eyes or the other way around. His skin was the wrong color. I wanted to ask him to open his eyes, please see me once. Or forget about me, just look at her one more time, tell her something. I don't even care if you don't say a word to me but tell her you'll wait for her, she shouldn't hurry, she'll be okay here without you. Because I saw how she was looking at him, as if she wanted to follow, and I couldn't let her. That was one thing I knew. Tell her, I thought.

I went into the cold corridor. A young bald man was limping along on a cane. His eyes were blue—too blue, radioactive. He had long eyelashes, starry, as if they were wet. He didn't look at me. I reached into my wallet for my phone card. There wasn't anyone to call, really. Not Smoke. Maybe Thorn with his eyelashes like the bald man's, his magician's bouquet. But when I dialed his number in Berkeley, an answering machine came on, with a woman's voice saying they weren't there, leave a message. She was every woman I'd seen when I was with him, every beautiful woman. I saw her lying on a bed full of roses he'd picked for her. He had pulled off each prickle; maybe his hands bled a little when he did it but he'd been so thorough that she could roll across them and no scratch would mar her perfect—peach or gold or was it teak-colored?—skin. Why did I think I could call Thorn now? I'd left him, hadn't I? I had left him.

My mother never left my father's side. Maybe she was silently chanting spells, incantations. Maybe she believed her magic could bring him back. But two days later the doctor told her it was time, there wasn't a chance anymore. She didn't cry. She let me hold her hand as we walked out of the hospital.

I bought some carrot juice and avocado sandwiches from the health food market down the street. I drove my mother to a park and we sat on the sparse grass in the sun and I tried to make her eat. She hadn't eaten since he'd gone into the hospital. She looked almost as thin as I was now. I thought, she looks like my little sister. My tall, beautiful little sister. I wanted her to comfort me but that was what I was supposed to do.

When we got back home I opened all the windows to air out the rooms. I picked some flowers from the garden and made green tea and lit candles. I ran a bath for my mother and put in lavender salts. My mother said, "There's something for you. In his studio."

I thought, what if it's the painting he's been promising me. Ever since I moved back from school he'd been saying he was going to paint me. Maybe he'd been doing it in secret from sketches he'd made while I slept. Me in my grandmother Rose's wedding dress. Maybe it was waiting for me, his good-bye.

My father's studio had been a greenhouse once. One big green glass wall overlooked my mother's terraced flower beds. The whole room had a soft garden light. It was chilly and smelled of turpentine. There was a canvas on an easel, a palette smeared with dried gobs of paint and some brushes soaking in a glass. My father had just painted the background of the canvas—a celestial blue. I wondered what he had meant to add. Maybe it was finished.

The wooden box was sitting on a table beside a jar of dried roses and some seashells—iridescent abalone, a rippled pink conch, something I didn't recognize that looked like human bone. My name was painted on the box. I held it for a long time. I didn't want to open it. This little box couldn't contain all I needed from him.

But inside were his best paints, some tubes hardly touched. Cadmium yellow, cerulean blue, yellow ochre, alizarin crimson, titanium white, ultra violet. And there were brushes, silky brushes of every size and shape, some so tiny they reminded me of eyelashes. Pale green artists' pencils with freshly sharpened silvery graphite tips. There was a new little palette and a sketchbook of the finest handmade paper.

The only painting in the studio, besides the blue canvas, was the skeleton, mired in thickly smeared oils. I went and stood in front of it. I said, "I wanted him to see me, Mister Bones."

Bones grinned at me. *Maybe Echo is not meant to be seen.*

She is meant to see.

The White Horse

THERE WAS A FIRE SOMEWHERE. FIRST, THE charred smell. Then the pieces of ash like peeled flesh. The wind blew them up against the windshield. Gray smoke from under the bridge. She wondered if the house were on fire. When she got off the freeway—home—she would run into his bedroom and let the flames seal it up.

"As a people we had to choose faith over anguish," he had told her. "Otherwise we would all have perished from grief when it happened. But I had no faith until you." He was lying in bed, wearing the silk cap she had made him, his hair mostly gone from the treatments. "We will always have each other, Eva."

Now there is nothing, she thought. She who had always had faith in everything. Trees feathers babies rivers iris light. Now there was only the torn ash in the air. Cars all hot chrome burning on the freeway and the smoke coming up from underneath. Nothing to go home to except the canned soups and crackers she had started eating, the bottles of gin. Days of pulling things out of closets, putting them in piles, putting them back. The hours it took to do the dishes, boiling them clean of fear. He was wrong about them always having each other. He was gone. Maybe she would go home to find the house had burned down.

But it had not burned. Mister Bones was hanging above the fireplace. She made herself shower and put on a black dress her daughter had left behind when she moved out. The party was at Natalie and Stephan's. They had been his colleagues at the university and she recognized most of the people from the few functions she had attended. He never cared much for going out, always preferred to be home alone with her.

"Eva, you look beautiful." Natalie handed her a cocktail. "As always."

She knew this wasn't true. Not that it had been something she'd ever worried about but she knew how much she'd changed, almost overnight. And yet, Natalie seemed serious. Maybe the starved and charred look of her mourning was considered fashionable. She thought she looked like an Auschwitz survivor. Both she and her daughter living out his past this way.

She took the last sip of alcohol, feeling the burn that she had always hated before.

"I'll go get you another." Natalie ran off and she stood alone, her hands like ice from the glass.

There was a man watching her. She was used to men's eyes but there had always been her husband's love like a screen surrounding her. This man's flesh, stretched taut over high cheekbones and angular chin, was the color of something she had seen today—yes, the ash blown on the freeway. His eyes were light, mesmerizing.

"I've seen you before," he said.

No, she would have remembered his pallor, his bones, his strange light eyes. "I don't think so."

"I know." The man's lips slipped over his teeth. "It

looks like you need a drink. May I?"

She shook her head but he took her hand anyway. His palm felt frosty even against her own chill. The veins in his arms had a thorny blue glow. He led her to the bar and grabbed a bottle of gin, pouring it, straight, into a paper cup. It flared electric in her head and he was watching her. His eyes were like full-blown poppies, like sleep.

"It was at a gallery opening. I was a student of his."

She felt herself pulled toward him, falling.

"Come home with me, Eva." His voice cracked tenderly. "If you want. I'll just hold you if you want."

"Yes," she found herself whispering.

His room smelled of the burning, the smoke that had filled her on the freeway. Burnt hair, scented candles and tobacco.

On the walls were black-and-white drawings of emaciated, hairless men and women with sunken eyes. She went over to the bookcase and took out a heavy volume, opened it to some black-and-white photographs of heaps of bones. She looked back at the shelves, dizzy.

All the books were about the same subject.

"It's my specialty," he said. "I have studied it since I was a child. That's how I met him. I especially admired his early work. I knew that was his influence even before I read about his life."

She was shivering now.

"Before he met you. It is so fascinating, don't you think? Do you know what the word means? Well, of course you must, Eva. The wife of the expert."

A sacrifice consumed by fire.

"It sounds like it refers to some kind of natural disaster. Or unnatural. Holocaust. But it is a sacrifice. They were sacrificed. For what do you think? Fascinating."

The sudden sound of wings, but a sound like flesh on flesh, not feathers brushing, startled her. A black bird was perched on a metal stand above the bed. The terror of birds she had felt ever since the illness bit at her intestines. She had always loved birds before—they had come to her, to ornament her and sing her songs and eat from her hand. But there had been ravens in the bushes around the hospital. A pigeon trapped in the house, shuddering against the glass again and again. Dreams of vicious birds with hooves and teeth.

The man took her, caught her lips like slices of meat. He burned like ice cubes. A searing jolt of numbness. A slick ointment. She wanted his poison. A sleep without dreams. The bird's throat made a savage sound.

"Why would he want to be cremated after what happened to his people?" she heard the voice say. "He abandoned his religion for you. You became his religion."

When she woke the man was asleep beside her. Her eyes ached dry and her mouth was sore and cracked at the corners. She stood up, her head and stomach swerving with nausea. Slowly she walked to her car. An animal lay in the road, flattened and bloodless as the thing that was supposed to be beating in her chest.

When she got back to the house, the light was whitish lavender and a bird was singing. She stood in the garden that was only weeds now. One veiny iris bloomed in the tangle. Once he had said, "Flowers are reincarnation. They come out of the earth of our ashes. Nothing else looks so soul-like." She had worked in this garden for hours to give him the souls to paint.

The garden of weed and he was not there. A disappearance. He was away. That was all. How else to explain?

There were no flowers anymore. But the iris had appeared overnight. She knelt in the earth before it. "They come out of the earth of our ashes," the flower whispered.

She pressed her lips to its round head and felt it tremble. She fit her whole mouth around and it seemed to stiffen with excitement.

When she looked up the white horse was standing there as if the fog had taken this shape. His muscled moon-silver body. His toss of mane and tail. The long shivery slope of his nose. She moved toward him as slowly as possible, holding her breath. In that dream-time she didn't question how he could be here; all she knew was that she needed to touch him. She put out her hand and he hesitated, a tremor passing through both of them, before he reached out and nuzzled her. He was warm and she felt the delicate jets of the breath through tremulous nostrils, the bristling hairs, the hard strength of teeth beneath the furl of his lip. His eyes were what made her know. The big dark brown tender light-filled orbs that were the eyes of her husband.

Psycho pomp. Spirit guide.

She remembered standing on the cliff with her daughter, scattering the ashes over the sea. When they got home she said, "I'm not sure I can go on without him." She hadn't meant to say it. Echo had grabbed her shoulders. "No, I need you." Her girl, her best flower, her sad mermaid. Remember when her hair was green at seventeen? Remember twelve dancing through the house like a force of nature? Cascading flood raging fire. Remember eight when she made the valentine with the antique lace doily and the tiny round mirrors—remnants from a skirt from India—and the pressed flowers? For the most wonderful mother in the world. You are our angel. No, baby, not an angel. "You can't leave, Mom." She had wanted to stay and help her daughter, give her love to the one who was living but she was so tired without him.

And why had he chosen this? Ashes. So she had become ashes with nothing left inside of her. No gardens feasts healing love. Her mind empty. Except for some dim thoughts of needing to sleep.

Now she did not want to sleep. She would call Echo. She would feed her. Wasn't Echo too thin still? Too pale. Was she smoking cigarettes? Eva thought she'd smelled them in her daughter's hair. What was Echo feeling? Did she know how much her father had loved her? Maybe she was afraid to know, just as he had been afraid to show her. He was gone now. Would it make it only hurt her more? Would she hear it if her mother told her? And was it true, or something Eva wished were true? But they would talk. Echo always knew so much about everyone else. Maybe she would come and dance, see inside Eva the way she had seen when she was in the womb, all-knowing. Maybe she would see the story of the man with the black bird, the appearance of the white horse.

Eva and Echo would light candles on the Sabbath as Eva's mother had done when she was a child, with the white lace on her head, saying the blessings. She wanted to sink herself wrist-deep into the soil to prepare for flowers. Every day her tears would water the lawn. The horse would stay at her side, nuzzling her neck, nibbling food from her palm, gazing into her eyes. She would ride him through the hills at twilight. She would scrub her skin and rinse out her mouth until Death's stinging numbing ointment was gone. She would take down the painting of Mister Bones.

And the lawn would not burn, the house would not burn—no, she would not go back to the man.

Skye

AFTER MY FATHER DIED I STARTED TO PAINT
again. He had taught me how to stretch the canvas and
prepare it with gesso, how to make an eye alive with
a dab of white, lips ready to part with a gleam and a
shadow. I wanted him to know I hadn't forgotten. I
used the paints he had left me. I made faces, one after another—of the girls. But always with something a
little off. Bella's eyes have bars shadowing them, Linda
bites her hand, Jolie's mouth bleeds.

It wasn't enough. I wanted to be her—Beauty. Maybe
that was why things happened the way they did.

I was working at Iris, the gallery where my father used
to show his paintings. When I was little, the whole
street was lined with galleries and, on opening nights,

so crowded with collectors, bohemians and celebrities milling around, drinking white wine from plastic cups, that traffic was stalled for hours at a time. Now my father's gallery was the only one left. It was small and dimly lit. The only light came from the remaining paintings of my mother, although those were quickly disappearing. I sat at a tiny desk cataloguing and filing papers for the owner, Iris herself, a petite eighty-year-old actress who liked to waltz down her staircase dressed in her finery from half a century ago. She entertained me with monologues from Shakespeare and stories about the gallery's glory days. The gentle horror-movie actors, ballet gods with feet like hooves, and bohemian queens in long velvet scarves who were her favorite clients. I kept telling myself I was going to show Iris my paintings but I never did. She was the only person I spoke to all day. The rickety clack of the manual typewriter echoed through the gallery where my mother had once tamed the monsters in my father's paintings.

At night I went home to my apartment in Los Feliz. My rooms were lit all year with Christmas lights and hung with upside-down bunches of dried roses. I made myself a salad for dinner and drank mineral water with lime. Sometimes I thought of Thorn. He had written me a letter saying he had met someone. They were engaged. He hoped I was all right. I moved the plastic dove ring to a different finger but I didn't take it off.

It was getting harder and harder to paint. I told myself I needed to be around people, move my body, something.

I met Nina first. She taught aerobics classes at the gym and I used to stand next to her, looking at all those mysterious muscles—the arcs of her biceps, her ladder-like abdomen, tight rear end, strong, narrow quads, powerful calves. Everything tanned evenly. I wanted that perfection. Maybe, I thought, you can find it without starvation—with protein and sweat and pain becoming perfectly formed, taut body tissue.

She flirted with everyone, going around while we did sit-ups asking, "You all right, hon?" in her pleasure-promising voice. One time she patted my bare stomach. "You eating, girl?" she asked. I felt as if she had said she loved me.

And then one time we were alone in the Jacuzzi

together. Soft bluish light and the sound of the jets and my body was pulsing in the water. She was brown, beaded with wet, shiny. My father did a series of paintings of my mother in water once. She looked like pearls.

Nina asked me my name. She told me that I was doing really well, really committed.

I felt light-headed from the steam and her eyes on me. "You inspire me," I said.

"I'm glad. I hope I make you feel good," she said. "I just hope you're getting enough calories."

I told her I was working on it. I had already gained some weight. I asked how she got her body that way.

"My boyfriend helps. He's pretty tough on me. He says it's all a sacrifice. I mean anything really beautiful takes sacrifice. L.A. was a desert first and now look at it. And going into space. Mark says the *Challenger* crew were like a gift to knowledge, to understanding the universe.

"But you look like you know something about sacrifice," she said.

She tossed her dark hair and the ends, damp from the water, slapped against her dazzling shoulders as she rose from the steam. There was a bruise on her left hip showing through the tan where the skin was thin. She must have seen me flinch at that one imperfection because she looked down at it.

"He's crazy," she said. "A biter."

She laughed, wrapping herself in a thick, red towel. "See you next class."

The next week in the locker room she was disarmingly naked again, big breasts exposed, arms lifted above her head as she brushed her hair. I was asking her about the best foods to eat.

"I live on fish and brown rice and vegetables, but a lot of everything. Hardly any fats, though. There's this great restaurant in West Hollywood we always go to. Mark and I'll take you. He knows everything about that stuff."

I met them in the shady courtyard restaurant where tanned people sat discussing astrology or reading movie scripts. Nina wore a short black dress and the muscles in her calves were flexed even more than usual from the tilt of her high-heeled sandals. Her hair was slicked back and her mouth was very red.

"This is Mark."

He was huge, perfectly built, with the kind of skin that looks like the sun is shining from underneath it. His teeth were white, big.

The actor-handsome waiter came with menus and said, "Hi, you guys. I'm surprised you're here when Skye's off."

Nina smiled at him, stroking her shoulders like they were kittens. "I knew you'd give us free soup anyway, Charlie."

When he left, she told me, "Skye's my baby brother. That's with an *e*. He works here and always gets us free stuff. Well . . . he used to." She and Mark exchanged a look.

We ordered and the waiter brought carrot juice, miso soup, cold cold salads with grated vegetables, a basket of corn bread. Mark watched me while I ate.

"She's really pretty. Don't you think so, Nina?"

"I told you already," Nina said.

I looked down.

"I mean unusual looking, right? Not what you'd usually consider attractive but it works."

"I think you're embarrassing her," Nina said.

When his food came, he said, "Fish is the perfect food." He squeezed a lemon slice, lifted a pink segment of salmon with his chopsticks.

"But he eats steak, too," Nina said. "Really bloody. He just doesn't like to admit it."

"Once in a while flesh is great for you." He kept staring at her. "You should train," he said. I realized he was talking to me. "You have a cute little body. You could get to be really amazing. Nina looked like you before she met me. Kind of anorexic."

"We'll help you," Nina said.

They both turned to look at me.

We started the next week. I'd sit in the outer-thigh press machine leaning forward, straining, with Mark kneeling between my legs, my hands on his shoulders. Nina would stand with one hip thrust out, telling me to breathe. Or I'd be on my stomach, curling up my calves to work the hammies as Mark called them, while they stood on either side of the machine watching me, touching my butt sometimes. Then I'd lie on my back while Mark separated and pushed open my thighs, helping me to stretch.

"It's important to stay flexible. The quad muscles can get so strong that if lightning struck, they could go into spasms and break the bones."

After training we'd go out to eat or sometimes to the Venice boardwalk to watch the bodybuilders and skaters, lick nonfat frozen yogurt, get our fortunes told, work on our tans. Not that I ever got brown like they did. My skin freckled and burned.

I don't know what it was, why I needed them. Maybe because they made me feel visible. I didn't question anything. I was bored with my life, with the gallery, my tiny apartment, too bored to paint anymore, always tired and ravenous except when Mark and Nina were around.

One night after training we went out for sushi and sake. Mark ordered for us and we tried all different kinds of fish—translucent, firm, glossy pieces on neat beds of rice. Mark and Nina had a contest to see who could handle the most wasabi. They gobbed the pale green stuff into their mouths until their eyes teared. We laughed, sipping the rice wine that seemed to shine in our throats. Nina kept leaning up against me, giggling, her hair getting in my face. I felt her breasts pressing. Mark sat watching us quietly, his fingers wrapped around his sake cup. I saw the veins standing out in his tan neck.

After, we went to a bar in Silverlake and drank shots of tequila and danced. We were wet from tequila sweats, flinging our bodies around in the spill of lights. Wasted. When we left the bar Nina leaned on me, hot skin and cold red silk. She looked up at the full moon.

"It must have been so mysterious before they went there," she said. "Now it's just dust."

Mark came between us, putting his big hands on our shoulders. I felt the current created by our bodies. The wires buzzed. You could almost see blue electricity racing between telephone poles above us, almost smell it.

"Like everything, baby," he said.

They lived in an apartment building called the Isis. It had lotus-shaped columns in front and a lot of orange trees weighed down with fruit. Their room was all bed, dominated by this massive bed that became more and more beds reflected in the mirrors on the walls. On the walls, where there weren't mirrors, were photos of parts of lean tan bodybuilder bodies. It took a while to figure out what was what—knee or shoulder, breast or hip. Mark lit candles. It seemed like a thousand candles. There was music playing—something that gave me a thrilled feeling in my throat and at the nape of my neck.

Nina sat on the bed, took a hand mirror and looked into it, pursing her lips. She held it up to me.

"What do you see in there?"

Lit by candles I saw myself beautiful. I touched my hair. My nipples showed through the silk shirt Nina had lent me. She had said I needed to start wearing new clothes, all my vintage stuff was ghosts.

Mark came over and sat between us. He took the mirror from me and set it on knees that strained the fabric of his jeans. He emptied the coke onto the mirror, making a perfect razor-sharp line with it, gesturing to me. I bent down and inhaled. It sparked through me like exploding crystals, white fireworks. I looked down at my face resting on Mark's knees. My eyes were candles.

Nina inhaled. She sat up, tossing her hair, blinking. The candlelight shone on her brow bone, her lower lip.

"Tell us a story, Mark," she said. I could hear the breath in her voice.

He was gazing into the mirror at his face and the line of white powder. He leaned over and inhaled.

"A story? You want a story?"

"Tell us. Tell us a story about Echo."

He didn't look away from his face. He touched his hair.

"Once there was a girl who loved a beautiful boy but he wouldn't pay any attention to her. He was in love with this girl he saw in a pool of water. He would sit staring at this girl all day long. The girl who loved him went crazy and died and the boy was turned into a flower. He didn't realize he had been in love with his reflection. The Greeks told that, right, Echo? I think it was really about the blood sacrifices they used to make to the gods. To nature. The boy's too beautiful, dies, becomes a flower. There's blood sacrifice in almost every great culture."

Mark looked up at me, took my face in his hands.

Nina came and knelt at my feet. I felt her fingers un-
buttoning my shirt. I was reflected in the mirrors. I was
reflected in their eyes.

I woke with a hangover in my own bed. They must
have brought me home but I couldn't remember. My
muscles felt waterlogged. I looked at myself in the mirror. Something had changed. My skin glowed the way
my mother's always did, my eyes looked lit up and I
was shaking. I tried to eat something but my stomach
clenched so I drank some hot water with lemon out of
a rattling cup and slept all day with the curtains shut.

I wanted Mark and Nina but I didn't want them. I
didn't go to the gym and I let my answering machine
pick up every time the phone rang. Nina was the only
one who called, leaving a message saying she and Mark
wanted to take me out again soon. I erased her voice.
She called again, saying, "Why aren't you at the gym?
Mark says you don't want to lose that muscle tone and
get fat. Call me, girlfriend."

I didn't want them but I wanted them. I dreamed
of our bodies impossibly tangled under water, writh-

ing in seaweed and tentacles, cut by jagged shells, our blood marbling the water. I dreamed of my toes becoming the roots of a tree, my arms extending, growing leaves, becoming branches, my hair a bouquet of fruit blossoms. I woke up and the sheets were wet with sweat. My muscles felt so heavy I could hardly get up and the cramps in my stomach made it impossible to eat anything except a light vegetable broth. But I thought about food all the time. Muscles and bones and blood pleading: steak, sweet potatoes, buttery corn-on-the-cob, quarts of vanilla-bean ice cream, pizza, pancakes, grilled pink salmon steaks. I remembered Mark eating his salmon that first day, his big chewing teeth, moist lips. I thought of the restaurant. Maybe I'd see them there. I'd better not go, I thought. I didn't want to see them. I wanted them. I'd better not go.

The waiter looked like Nina. But Nina without the tan—a younger, pale Nina with dark circles under the eyes. He moved gracefully among the tables like a deer in a forest. There was something hunted about him. When he came over with the menu he smiled. His eyes crinkled up and he had deep dimples that looked more like lines because his face was so lean.

I asked if he was Nina's brother.

The smile disappeared. "Yes," he said.

"I'm a friend of Nina and Mark's."

I noticed how thin the skin was over the bridge of his nose and the top of his cheekbones, almost translucent, lightly freckled. Those dark circles under his eyes.

"How did you meet them?" he asked when he brought my food.

I told him about the gym. For some reason I kept talking. I told him my dad had died recently, I had dropped out of school at Berkeley, was working at an art gallery. I told him how much better I'd been feeling since I started working out. At first. Maybe I was hitting some kind of plateau. . . .

When I finished eating he said, "I'd really like to see you again, where we could talk."

I wrote my name on a napkin and gave it to him. Before I left he looked right into my eyes. I thought of Nina's and Mark's eyes like mouths ready to eat my breasts and legs. Then Skye's eyes disappeared into

twinkling crinkles as he smiled and he shook my hand.
He had a warm, dry, firm grip.

"I'll call you," he said.

He called the next night and I lay on my bed as the
sky darkened, talking to him. The air smelled of the
fires that had been burning out of control, and of
flowers—honeysuckle and mock orange. Skye asked
me about the gallery. I hadn't talked about art since I
dropped out of school. Klimt's lovers, sex suggested under a fall and pattern of gold mosaic. Picasso's Blue and
Rose periods. Botticelli angels. The Rodin museum in
Paris. My favorite Rodin was the *Danaide*, lying on her
side with her hair over her face. You could tell by her
sinuous back and her hair that she was weeping. Also,
The Cry. She had her mouth open; you could hear the
scream. She reminded me of a fish woman who had
been pulled from her water.

"There's this whole world I want to see. I forget
sometimes. I can't breathe here," he said.

"Can you see the moon?" I asked watching it rise
outside my window.

"They can't make it stop."

"Stop what?"

"Glowing," he said as if he were speaking in his sleep.

We went out on the third of July. I wore a cream-colored silk 1920s dress that I had gotten for a few bucks at a flea market. I didn't care if it was haunted.

Skye came to the door looking like a pale Nina. I asked him in while I finished getting ready and when I came out of the bathroom he was standing in front of one of my Beauties.

"Is this yours?"

I nodded. "I haven't done many lately."

"Can I see more?" And I showed him.

He stood and looked at each one for a long time. Then he looked into my eyes. "You should start again."

I shrugged. I wanted to get away from the pictures.

We ate at an old Italian restaurant on Hollywood Boulevard. Skye took a roll from under white linen, cracked the gold crust, buttered the soft inside, handed it to me over the red candle. My stomach was better. He ordered angel hair pasta for us.

"So you work out with my sister."

I nodded and he was silent, frowning into his plate.

"It helps release tension," I said, like I had to explain. "It makes me feel better about myself."

"You sound like me. I used to work out with them. I was trying to do the acting thing. I started training with them but then I realized how obsessive it was. That was my life. It's cool to work out but those guys are obsessed." He paused. "You have a lot of other reasons to feel good anyway. Like your painting."

"Are you acting now?"

"Not commercially. When it comes to losing a part because your eyes are the wrong color, trying to flirt with everyone to get commercial work you don't want that much anyway . . . it kind of made me sick."

"So what now?"

"I don't know. I'm trying to figure it out. I want to do some theater. I'd like to just live, I guess."

After we'd eaten he got up, took my hand, danced me around in front of the bar while an old man in a red vest played piano. It was late and the restaurant was

empty. Skye's hair smelled of smoke, corn bread and leaves.

We drove to Santa Monica in his beat-up pickup and walked in the park on the cliffs overlooking the water. Some homeless people slept in the pale green wood latticework gazebo or on the damp grass. A man staggered up to us, asking for change. Skye gave him a few bucks, looking straight into his eyes.

"It blows me away to see how people live in this city," he said, his mouth twisting. "This oasis."

We were quiet for a while, walking. I could smell the ocean and it reminded me of how, once, I had wanted to step off the oasis and find another one beneath that churning surface.

"I get so hungry here," I said. "Do you know what I mean? Not just physically."

"There's not much that's very nourishing."

I thought about my job at the gallery, the gym, my mother riding a white horse through the hills, believing it was my father. And wasn't I just as bad, pretending I had forgotten but still waiting for a boy who would never come? Maybe if I got away from this city for a while. Painted again.

Skye turned to me and I saw him very white and almost fragile-looking in the moonlight.

"I know we don't even really know each other but I just think you should be careful with this thing with my sister and Mark. It really fucked me up. I just think you should think about it."

I asked him what he meant and he shivered, hunching into his denim jacket. "Just be careful, okay?"

We stayed there a long time. People started arriving with the pinkish streaks of light to see the fireworks at dawn. We stood against the railing looking out over the pier as the sky exploded with fire flowers. He put his arm lightly around my shoulders.

When we got back to my apartment my heart was pounding. I asked him in and went to the bathroom to wash my face. In the mirror I saw that my eyes were glazed and circled with shadows and my makeup was smudged. My skin looked blotchy. As I stood there staring at myself, feeling a queasiness in my stomach, there was knock on the half-open door and Skye came in. He stood behind me, reflected in the glass.

"Your paintings are amazing," he said. "You shouldn't

need Mark and Nina to make you feel beautiful."

I wanted to dance for him then so he could see me, really see. And so I could see him. My hand went to the buttons of my dress, hesitated; our eyes met again in the mirror.

He reached for my wrist. I turned to him, running my free hand through his soft hair. Then my fingers traveled along the side of his face to his throat. I un-buttoned his shirt collar, feeling the warmth. He pulled away. On the smooth, pale skin of his neck I saw a scar—precise, painful looking, the memory of some deep fruitlike wound. But he had pulled away. Had I really seen it?

"Skye?" I said. I shut my eyes and there was an image of three bodies tangled on a bed. Two men and a woman. Candlelight. Mirrors. Blood flower-ing the sheets. *There's blood sacrifice in almost every culture.*

He turned and I followed him out of my bathroom to the front door.

"Be careful, Echo," he said. Then he left.

I went back into the bathroom and undressed. I

took a bath, tenderly soaping my body. I got into bed, held myself as I fell asleep.

I waited for two weeks, hoping he would call. Then I went by the restaurant during his shift but he wasn't there. I called but they said he'd quit. He wasn't listed in the phone book.

I called Nina.

"Where've you been?" she sounded cold.

"I've just been really tired lately," I said. "I haven't been feeling too well. Nina, I called to ask for your brother's number."

"What?" I could hear her breathing through her nostrils. "Skye? You met him? Don't tell me you're all into Skye."

"Could you just give me his number?" Suddenly I didn't care what she thought.

"Listen, girlfriend, my brother's sick. He has a blood disease. And he's always getting people involved with him and then just cutting them off. Just forget about Skye. You have enough of your own problems."

"He has what?"

"Something's wrong with his blood. They're doing tests. I can't believe you got yourself involved with Skye."

"I need to talk to him, Nina. Where is he?"

"Forget it," she said. "Listen, Mark and I are working out tonight and getting dinner. You should come. You'll feel better." The pleasure voice again. As if I'd been forgiven for now.

"Aren't you worried about him?"

"Skye has his own life, okay? He used to be really close to Mark and me but now we don't talk. He's crazy. I mean, it's sad he's sick but you know just because he's my brother doesn't mean I have to like him."

I hung up.

That night I dreamed about Mark. I was standing naked in front of him wanting to dance for him to see inside him and he wouldn't look at me. He was staring into a mirror and nothing stared back. I woke up shaking. I knew I needed to see Mark and Nina again one more time.

"I heard about this guy who went insane. He got into his orange trees so much he went to the hospital and bought human blood for the soil," Mark said, tearing a segment of orange and putting it into Nina's mouth with his long fingers.

"No way, Mark. Someone made that up because of the name of those kind of oranges."

"It's true."

"I don't believe it. Hospitals don't just sell blood like that."

"Maybe he got it some other way."

"You are sick sometimes, Mark."

I was sitting with Mark and Nina on the lawn above the sea. It was dark after a sunset where the sun hung low in the sky like one of Mark's blood-bred oranges. The moon was rising. Nina caressed her shoulders and Mark turned to her. His teeth were white in the moonlight, big, violent.

"Don't you want to be beautiful, Echo? My little blood orange like Nina."

He leaned toward her. I knew the wound would be as fruitlike as the one on Skye's throat. I tried to scream, but it was like in a dream where nothing comes out.

Nina saw the look in my eyes. She just smiled.

Shivering on the bus that would take me home, I knew I would never see them again. And Skye was gone. In my apartment I took out my paints, my canvas, squeezed some color onto the palette my father had given me. A painting of beauty. Maybe not a woman this time. Maybe a crystal, a light, an explosion of lights, a tree covered with suns. The paint I squeezed out was wet and red like blood but it was only paint. A different sacrifice to a different beauty.

Eden

WHEN SHE WAS FIFTEEN EDEN DECIDED TO HAVE
the operation. If she didn't have it, eventually she might
not be able to dance, or even walk. There had been some
damage to her spine when she'd had the earlier surgery
as a little girl and it needed to be corrected now. There
was the possibility that something could go wrong and
leave her paralyzed but Eden was brave. Her mother
had raised her to face anything. When you are that sick
as a little child that happens. Either you can face anything. Or nothing. Eden was brave.

Eden was tall, with silvery blond hair to her waist
and deep-set silver-blue eyes and silvery veins beneath
her silver-white skin. She still had the torso of a child,

which she tried to disguise with padded bras that were always a bit big. Her small breasts made her cry sometimes. But no boy cared about their size for they saw her hair, her skin, her long graceful limbs. She had a set of acrylic fingernails applied to make her long delicate hands seem even longer. She painted the nails vermilion. People stared at her on the street and in restaurants and inquired if she were a model. She had a tiny cleft in her chin and a devilish curl to her full lips.

When Eden was eleven her mom Wendy and her dad Jeff moved to Colorado. They had a pretty little cottage by a rushing creek. The air was good for Eden's delicate lungs. Secretly, at the age of thirteen, she was able to rationalize her smoking habit better than if she still lived in L.A. They had kitties and puppies, goats, chickens and llamas, an organic vegetable garden. Wendy and Jeff opened a health food restaurant. Eden went to school and all the boys worshipped her from afar. She was planning on returning to L.A. one day and becoming a singer-songwriter, a techno Joni Mitchell. She took singing lessons and piano, wrote song lyrics. She took ballet classes three times a week and went dancing with her friends on weekends. She loved to dance. It reminded her of being onstage as a little girl, of the love she felt coming up from the audience and the love shining inside of her, able to express itself through the movements of her limbs. Then Eden found out she had to have the operation if she hoped to dance again.

She talked to her mom's friend Smoke the night before she went into surgery. Eden hadn't seem him in years but he always sent her birthday presents and called occasionally. She flirted with him on the phone.

"Do you have any girlfriends yet?" she always asked and he always said, "No, sweetie." And she'd say, "Are you saving yourself for me?" and he'd scold her for being such a flirt. Then she'd reply, "It's because I'm stuck here in Colorado without any rock stars to keep me company. When are you coming to visit us?"

She had a picture of herself as a little girl onstage with him. He was so sexy and she could tell he loved her. This night, the night before the operation, he said quickly, like trying to get it over with, "Yes, there's somebody but it's not serious," when she asked about girlfriends and she said, "Who?" trying to sound excited and he said, "You know her but you probably don't remember. She met us when you were little. Her name is Echo."

Eden did remember, of course she did. She had predicted this a long time ago. She remembered how Echo had held her hand and danced with her, drawn the mermaid on her cast. Eden knew she was falling in love with Smoke, like all the girls but maybe more. And then, later, Eden had seen her again at a nightclub, looking much thinner, looking so sad, and Eden had tried to get Smoke to go up to her but he hadn't wanted to. She was happy for him, now, that he'd finally found someone, happy for Echo, too. But by the way he acted after, Eden could tell he wished he hadn't told her.

She held the picture of herself and Smoke against her chest on the wheelchair ride to the operating room. It was the thing she focused on as they put her under— the rose-colored light and the spangled tulle and gauze and his deep spinning blue eyes.

He came as soon as Jeff called him. Eden's lungs had collapsed during the operation.

"Wendy needs you. She just keeps saying your name

over and over again," Jeff said, trying not to remember the way he'd felt onstage with Wendy and Smoke, as if he didn't exist. That was years ago and she was his now, he told himself, pregnant with his child. All that mattered was helping her and the baby get through this. And Eden.

So Smoke flew in from Los Angeles where he was living in an apartment in Los Feliz with Echo. Smoke was pretty broke so Echo paid for the ticket. She offered to go with him but he said he needed her to stay and take care of things. He'd call her and let her know. Jeff met him at the airport and they sped to the hospital through the ice. Every crystal on the windshield was daggerlike.

Wendy had spoken to a psychic after Eden's lungs collapsed. The psychic had said, "Everyone you know is taking a little of her pain on themselves. There's a man who needs to come see her. He owes her something from another life. He will take her pain."

"JJ," Wendy said and she went back into the tiny dark hospital room where Eden lay like Sleeping Beauty in red Converse high-tops and a metal halo, struggling to breathe. The picture of her and Smoke was on the wall along with all the recent pictures of her dancing and mugging with her friends. Wearing her baggy clothes and with her hair in cornrows or pigtails or flying loose around her head like feathers. Wendy had put the pictures there to remind the nurses of who was beneath the metal and tubes. Smoke came into that room and he was white as Eden's hospital sheets and he was shaking and his blue eyes were like gas flames. He touched Wendy's hand and she looked up and breathed again for the first time it seemed since this had happened, shallow and rough but a breath. She hadn't left Eden's side the whole time, only to call people and use the restroom. She hadn't eaten or slept. She hadn't let Jeff or anyone else spell her but she let him.

He told her, "It will be all right," and he was so fierce electric blue that she let herself believe him, even with the whiteness of his fear.

He took Eden's cold frail hand and sat beside her in the darkness. She was wearing the cast for her spine with the metal halo around her head. He noticed her long red nails, which had been applied the day before the surgery. He noticed the many piercings—her nose, her ears—but they'd made her remove the jewels. Somehow she'd managed to keep on the tiny pink crystal anklet he'd sent her. It fit and he realized he always thought of a little child when he bought her gifts; her bones were still that small around but long now and she had curving hips and of course that womanly face that she'd always had—even as a baby, startling—though the eyelids hid her eyes and he wished so much he could see them. Even this way she was so beautiful it was like crystals of snow inside of him and then those Converse sneakers—it made him want to fall to his knees and scream for her to come all the way back.

"Do you hear me, Eden?"

He thought he saw her eyelids flutter and he put on the Enya tape he'd brought; he knew it was her favorite. He stayed at her side for so long he couldn't tell how many days had passed. He mostly just sat, playing the tape again, holding her hand. Then sometimes he would speak of how she would get better, how they would swim with dolphins, dance under stars and how she would wear glass slippers and be worshipped on a stage made of moonlight. He drew pictures of her as she lay there and he wrote songs that he sang to her and pages of poetry and even in his grief he was so grateful just to be at her side like this, leaving only to run down to the cafeteria for coffee when Wendy came. He'd walk through the hospital full of dying children and they would smile sometimes, comforting everyone whose worried faces they saw: *Yes, I'll be all right.* The kids in wheelchairs—bald, missing limbs, with their far-seeing eyes reflecting a light that wasn't the fluorescent hospital because that is what so many sick children learned to do. Maybe out of their deep kindness. Maybe afraid that otherwise everyone would leave. It was what his Eden had done—*see me smile, see me put on lipstick see me dance I am happy you mustn't be so afraid, afraid enough to leave.*

"But I left you, didn't I baby?" he breathed. "I left you thinking it would save us and now look what has happened."

Wendy told him what the psychic had said. Wendy had come to bathe Eden and she and Smoke sat together first for a long time whispering in the darkness.

Beautiful Wendy just a little fuller and a few lines

around her eyes but otherwise the same except she was Jeff's now, the way he'd always wanted it, and pregnant with his child, her breasts starting to get the way they had been with Eden.

"I do owe her," Smoke said.

"I shouldn't have told you."

"No. Yes you should."

Later, when he thought about it, he knew what it meant.

"Take me instead," he said to the darkness. "Take me instead of her. Take my soul and put it in this body. Let Eden go back to Echo and live in the pale yellow apartment building lit with Christmas lights all year, hung with upside-down bunches of dried roses and Echo's paintings, and she can stay there and make art and music and love."

Echo was weeping whenever he called her and she wouldn't say anything; she just cried and said give them my love and he told Echo how Eden was but really he was looking forward to getting off the phone and going back into the dark disinfected room with his baby.

It seemed to go on and on, this time together of

dolphins and goddesses and moonlight and flowers and crystals and angels and grief and terror and weeping and then finally Eden opened her eyes and stared at him—her deep-set silver-blue eyes and they were full of flirting right away and his heart clenched with joy and she whispered, "Smoky," and he said, "Hi, baby."

Eden told him, struggling to take each breath, "I was in this tunnel and they were on one end with their rainbow wings and you were on the other calling me. They were so beautiful but you are stronger."

He left a week later, the day Eden was released from the hospital. He kept telling himself, she is alive and I am still alive. What do I do now, so that she will still be safe? He went back to Echo. She met him at the airport with her leg in a cast. The day after he left she'd tried to stop her car from rolling into the one behind it at a gas station and her leg was caught. "You were helping take her pain," he said.

When they got home he and Echo made love but all he could think about was Eden. He showed Echo the poems and the drawings and a photograph of the fifteen-year-old beauty whom Echo still remembered as a skinny little child who had taken her hand in a nightclub as if wanting to protect her and could put on lipstick without a mirror, much better than she could with one. Echo was so relieved that Eden was okay but she kept crying, for a different reason now. She had understood from the first night she danced for him that Eden was his daughter and Echo also knew that he had not told her this partly because now it was an easier way to let her go. She wished her own father could have loved her the way Smoke loved Eden, even nearly as much.

Smoke wanted to tell Echo he loved her enough that he had wished for his baby's soul to come live with her forever in his body. Would she have understood? He didn't tell her.

Valentine

THE MOMENT I MET HER, I WANTED TO BE VALENTINE.
I was dancing by myself at a club when I saw her sipping her martini, watching me. I saw her as a little girl sitting at a booth with her dashing father. He was all shadows and light, chiaroscuro, like he'd stepped from a black-and-white movie. She was posing for his friends, learning how to flick her eyelashes and purse her lips around an olive. His perfect little doll until he died from the poison in his liver. That was when it became important that all the other men see her.

I stopped dancing. The music throbbed in my head like too much blood. I looked over at the red-haired woman with the tiny cartoon character poised on the edge of her glass.

Valentine smiled at me.

I'd drive up the canyon road to Valentine's magenta
adobe building under the Hollywood sign. In the evening the sky was jewelry colors from the sun and smog
and there was a harsh sweetness singeing the air. Bougainvillea, camellias, geranium and hibiscus flamed in
the gardens, pinker and redder in the moments before
darkness and the impending wash of chilly neon that
would make them pale.

L.A. is a beautiful prostitute with bougainvillea-
blossom-pink lips, hair extensions to her waist, stiletto
heels straining the muscles in her calves. Promising opiate dazzle if you pay her enough. And she doesn't just
want money.

Valentine and I would sit on her bed smoking
gold-tipped cigarettes, watching TV and eating greasy
take-out Chinese. If we were going to a club, Valentine would lend me a pair of 1950s rhinestone earrings
from the earring tree on her deco dresser. We called
it the tree because of the metal pieces sticking out like

branches and the earrings like candied fruits. Valentine would do my makeup, choosing the powdery shadows to bring out the gold rings she insisted she saw around my pupils.

"You'll make them crazy," she'd say. "We'll find you a love-boy tonight."

But I always felt almost invisible. Her red hair seemed to fill up the dark clubs like colored smoke. Men turned at the sight of that hair, cat eyes and a perfect body in black lace or blue sequins.

Valentine drank martinis like her father. She told me he had been an animator. He had created a character named Teenie Martini, a miniature girl who appeared on the rim of this guy's glass whenever he drank too much.

"There's no one worth our time here," she'd say, draining her drink, and we'd leave the maraschino-poison-cherry-red vinyl booth and the walls hung with dead movie stars, our pockets stuffed with the crispy fried noodles and fortune cookies they served. Sometimes we'd go to a fast-food Mexican place, like I used to do as a kid, eat burritos in Valentine's smoky

Studebaker Lark with the streetlights buzzing and glazing everything a greenish-white. Or the late-night Italian joint where she would peel the netting off of the red glass candle and slip it over her bare calf like a stocking. We'd drop crumpled fortunes on guys' plates on the way out and laugh; none of them were our loveboys.

Sometimes I wondered if I wanted one anymore, anyway.

We'd go to Valentine's apartment and watch horror movies on TV until we fell asleep. She couldn't sleep without the TV on. If she fell asleep first I'd look at her pale face, sometimes still masked with makeup, her violet lids and heart-shaped lips, and wish I could be her.

Valentine was obsessed with Mitch Kitteridge from the Bullets. Mitch seemed almost twice as tall as she was. He had slicked-back hair and large hands and large features and chilling eyes that could stun you with a glance. The Bullets played all the clubs and Valentine waited backstage, smoking hard. Then she'd follow Mitch around to a few parties. At dawn they'd go back to Mitch's.

"I don't need the TV on to sleep there," she told me. "He acts so tough and hard and cold and then we're alone, in the morning, he makes me Cream of Wheat. Mitch Kitteridge makes me Cream of Wheat!"

I'd never seen Valentine so happy or so beautiful as when she was with Mitch. She hennaed her hair again and bought fuchsia stilettos. Her skin was transparent and her lips were always a little parted. She looked like Teenie Martini, like a little cartoon character or a doll. One of those old-fashioned bisque ones with green glass eyes. Then Mitch stopped calling.

Valentine and I sat on her bed smoking and she talked and talked.

"I know he'll get over it . . . such a dick . . . oh well. He reminded me of my dad—strong silent type. If my dad was still alive I'd probably deal a hell of a lot better with these assholes."

"I know what you mean," I said.

"But he was so beautiful—that Cleo chick is a real airhead. He could never say I love you, though. He was always talking about other women's bodies. He drank too much. But then I just keep thinking of how he kissed me. And the cereal . . . It's so pathetic what will keep you coming back."

I looked at Valentine, powdery and obsessed, and saw the city was wearing her out. With its killing air and its zombie men and its terrible burning beauty. And wearing me out. Sometimes I thought the only reason I stayed was to find that boy who had rescued me from the ocean; I should have given up years ago.

"You need to get out of here," she said. We were watching *Night of the Living Dead* on TV and eating pot-stickers.

I had told her about Felice, a tall thin woman with big slanted yellow eyes who showed her huge cat sculptures at the Iris gallery. She had a place in the East Village that she wanted to sublet at a very cheap rate with the stipulation that I take care of her thirteen felines.

"Not that I know what I'll do without you."

"Come with me," I said.

But I knew she'd never leave. I think she thought she was Jean Harlow reincarnated as a redhead or something. There were pictures of Jean and Marilyn and James Dean on her wall. Hollywood Baby. Once she'd said, "If I ever committed suicide I'd jump the fuck off the Hollywood sign." She rubbed her bare and glitter-dusted arms and smiled a hazy smile.

I knew she'd never leave and that I'd never be Mitch Kitteridge for her. No matter what I did, I'd never make her feel like Teenie Martini. I could make her cereal but it wasn't the same; she'd never fall asleep in my arms without the TV on.

My mother was working in the garden, the white horse she believed was my father standing above her chewing his carrot, sheltering her from the sun so she didn't need a hat. His eyes were a lot like my father's I had to admit.

She stood up, wiping her hands on her jeans. She had started to wear jeans now, instead of the Indian gauze dresses my father liked, and she had cut her cascading hair short. She was just as beautiful as ever—a light shone out of her that reminded me of the crystals she still kept all over the house to catch the sun. She hugged me and I smelled crushed flowers. I felt like I couldn't breathe.

We went into the house. The air was coated with honey from the beeswax candles. We began to cook the Sabbath meal. My mother had started celebrating the holidays religiously since the night of the man and the black bird. On Passover when she set the wine out for the angel Elijah it disappeared and I know she didn't drink it herself because I kept my eye on her the whole time.

We made chicken soup and potato latkes with applesauce and sour cream. We made a large green salad and a side dish of peas, carrots and pearl onions. Chocolate macaroons. My mother had started eating sugar, which she had never touched when my father was alive. She even drank a little wine. She was writing a cookbook of the recipes, the ones she never used to write down and she'd already found a publisher. The book was full of mixed-up world cuisine—Japanese burritos with fresh seared tuna, sweet rice and wasabi; Greek pasta with olives, tomatoes and feta cheese; Jewish pizza with smoked salmon and cream cheese. She lit the candles at the table and said the blessing. She asked me how I was. I usually didn't tell my mother too many things about my life. I knew she would have worried if she'd known about the vampires and how a fairy almost died. I'd never told her how I'd once almost drowned or about the boy on the beach. But now I wanted to tell her about Felice and the apartment in New York and what Valentine had said and how I had decided to move away.

The white horse shuffled his hooves in his corner and looked at me with his liquid eyes. He was almost translucent in the light like a ghost. Even if he was my father it was hard to get used to having him inside. My mother took my hand.

"It's time for you to leave, isn't it?" she said.

I nodded. My eyes filled with tears. Maybe she knew, already, about Skye and Smoke and Eden and even the angel I'd once found on the beach. Maybe she was like me, able to see. I watched her face above the candles. My whole body hurt as if it were shrinking. I wanted to be able to fold back up inside her where I had come from. I wanted to be my mother. I wanted to be my red-haired bougainvillea Valentine in her magenta house, Teenie Martini perched on her glass. Thorn in his white cotton shirt doing magic tricks and writing poetry. I had wanted to be Eden. I think I had even wanted to be Smoke when I first saw him singing on that stage, when he kissed me and I remembered how he had made the most beautiful child whom he loved more than love, and how my father was gone and I was empty.

Valentine was in love with Mitch Kitteridge from the Bullets. Thorn had married the woman he met after I left; they were expecting their second baby. Smoke had moved to the desert. Boys worshipped Eden and she went out dancing every night. I had even glimpsed someone who looked just like Skye in a black-and-white European film about angels. They were all gone in their way but the only one I didn't know anything about was the boy on the beach.

I let my mother hold me against her breast where it was flowers and light and suffocation. I knew I had to leave.

Valentine drove me to the airport. She gave me a silver heart with wings of flame.

I moved into the tiny room with the thirteen cats and got a job as a waitress serving blue corn tamales and kiwi margaritas at a Caribbean restaurant/gallery decorated

with altars of roses and candles and spangled velvet wall
hangings. The owner, Rodrigo, was a swarthy man with
girlish hips who wore so much of his dead grandmother's
jewelry that it was a wonder he could lift his hands. One
night he pointed to Valentine's silver heart that I wore on
a long ribbon so it swung cool against my breasts when I
leaned over to serve my tables.

"Healing your heart?" he asked.

When I asked what he meant he said it was a milagro, a charm to heal the part of the body it represented.

On the days I wasn't working I walked around the city.
I walked all the way from the tiny stalls selling jewelry
and leather and platform boots, the Indian restaurants
and macrobiotic places in the Village, to the palatial designer shops, the sushi and French pastries on the Up-
per East Side. I never liked to take the subway, even
when my legs ached and numbing snow was falling. I
walked through the park with its zoo and its tunnels
and its pretzel and lemonade vendors and its runners
and its angel fountain. I went to the Metropolitan Museum every week and picked a room or two to devour.

I remembered when my parents took me to New York when I was little. I had been afraid of the subways and the crowds and the smell of garbage. Then my father took me to the Metropolitan Museum. I screamed and cried when he said it was time to leave. I had wanted to hide somewhere until it closed and live there forever. I had wanted to lick the paint on the Impressionist canvases and play in the Egyptian temple and sleep in the cool stone lap of the Buddha. My father had brought me back every day until we left New York. He said, "Someday maybe you will have your work in a museum." Now I knew I could almost live in the Metropolitan—I could go every day if I wanted.

On the way home I bought food from the little Korean market on the corner and started making elaborate meals without recipes. Sometimes they were disastrous and other times I called my mother to tell her my ideas for her cookbook. I ate seated on the floor with one candle and the thirteen cats. I spent rainy afternoons in bookstores, finishing whole novels before I knew it. But the best thing in my life were the art lessons. My teacher was a tiny blue-eyed Jewish man from Poland who looked Chinese and had known my father. When my money ran out he let me continue my lessons for free. I came to his loft overlooking the Hudson River. It was filled with ancient icons, a collection of bottles, broken teacups and tall green medicinal-smelling plants. We did some yoga poses together before we began.

"Paint your angels and your demons," he told me.

I painted Los Angeles. As soon as I'd gone away I remembered the watermelon sunsets, the fruits that seemed to fall from the sky, the neon flowers and petals of neon, the secret stone staircases and jungle gardens. In my mind the city was glowing. It was fanning its lights like a peacock. It was a tattooed diva singing torchy songs and dancing in the burnished gusts of Santa Ana winds. Its sheer dresses were catching fire and its hair was a flood and its hips were causing earthquakes but how beautiful she was.

It was a city of vampires and devils but named for angels and I had met one there. Sometimes I sent my watercolors to Valentine.

Valentine stayed in L.A., still working at a video production company. She went out at night searching for Mitch Kitteridge. Sometimes she'd have sex with a guy if he reminded her of Mitch, or if she was horny enough. She always made them leave the TV on so she could sleep. When she was depressed she went shopping for new shoes or lipstick. The shoes piled up in her room. Strappy sandals, stilettos, boots, pumps. At night it seemed to her as if they were dancing.

She called me on my birthday. I had spent it in the museum. Then I had taken myself to dinner at a Thai restaurant decorated in purple silk where they served rose petals in the salad, chunks of tofu with jasmine rice, hunks of sugared ginger, mangoes in coconut milk. I had bought myself some new art supplies and I was fondling them by candlelight when the phone rang.

Her voice was so soft I could barely hear it. My heart felt like the milagro—perfectly shaped silver, a healing charm.

"I'm sorry I didn't write a card. Things have been crazy."

I asked her what was wrong. I knew something was. Usually she would have called and just whispered, "Happy birthday, baby." She sounded tired.

"Everything's peachy except I got fired and they turned off the heat in my apartment, the one month it's cold in L.A., and I'm sitting here wearing three pairs of socks and three sweaters and freezing my ass off."

I asked what she was going to do. If she could stay with someone. I told her it shouldn't be too hard for her to find another job.

"I'm damn qualified but this is the worst season for hiring. I could stay with my mother but there is no way. I can't even really take a shower over there without dealing with her shit.

"This city is a bitch," she said. "You paint all the beauty. All the lights and peacocks or whatever. But now all I see is a bitch. This city is a bitch using people up. I've seen it destroy Jenny and my friend Pebbles and Adam but I thought, not me, you know?"

Jenny had had to be hospitalized because she had almost starved herself to death. She had taken it farther than I had. Valentine insisted it was caused by too many rejections from producers who said she wasn't young or sexy enough. Pebbles had been an amazing clothing designer who used stuffed animals and bones in her creations, the "It Girl" of the scene at seventeen until she got so screwed from drugs that now she was working in a garbage dump. Adam was a great guitar player—mind-blowing, Valentine said—who had

ODed a week after his band got their first record contract.

I asked Valentine to come stay with me. I told her again about my art teacher and the food I was learning to make and my walks through the city. How I'd finally stopped smoking. I told her about the shoes I saw in shop windows, glowing like magic talismans. How you always had an excuse to buy shoes here because of how much walking you did, not like in L.A.

She laughed and said she didn't need any excuses for shoes. She said, "Oh thank you, sweetheart, but I can't. I've got to work this all out."

I imagined her lying beside me under the antique wedding dress, her hair tickling my lips, her scent like all the pink and red flowers. I wanted to beg her but I didn't say anything.

Then one night, she called again.

She had just come out of the bathroom dressed in her peach satin kimono with the green dragon on it, and her green satin mules, and her French perfume, and she'd just had a martini in one of her Teenie glasses with her dad's little cartoon character inscribed on it in gold, and the phone rang.

It was an escort service she had signed up with one night when she was drunk and hungry and cold. They told her they had a customer for her. She was low on shampoo and soap and toilet paper and toast and milk. She said she'd go.

The hotel smelled of decay. The hallways were painted puke green.

The man was lying on the bedspread. She had a phobia about hotel bedspreads—who knew what went on on them and if anyone ever washed them. The man said, "You look like a Valentine." His breath smelled of stale beer and his gut was hairy and hanging. She told herself, a nice quick stash o' cash and then she'd get real work. She was damn qualified, wasn't she?

I thought of Valentine with her red hair and thin white coughing chest. Once I'd seen her slip a black lace cobweb of a top over that perfect sheen of skin. Dreamed of kissing her lips, as if that might let me become who she was.

The part that scared her was that afterwards, the

next night, they called her again. He had requested her.

"It was gross because I was flattered in a way," she said. "And I went and while he was doing it he started saying he loved me and crying. And that was what was really sick."

"You can come stay with me," I said. "Please, just come stay here."

"Oh you're sweet but I can't leave," she whispered. "I've got to work this all out."

And I saw her dressed in her silk dragon kimono, curled in her purple velvet love seat in her canyon apartment under the Hollywood sign. The round mirrors were all draped in black lace as if someone had died.

Once upon a time I wanted to be Valentine. Now I wanted to return, put the silver heart around her neck, rescue her, become her angel.

But I knew there were only peacocks outside her window. They would wake her in the morning. Those birds scream.

Wings

ECHO WENT DOWN INTO THE SUBWAY. SHE WAS no longer afraid of the rushing trains, the sunken tracks, the smell of urine, the dank air. She had spent the night in the Metropolitan Museum.

Echo hid in a stall in the ladies' room until it was quiet. Then she slipped out and wandered around all night. She felt as if she'd been in the secret temple of the gods, meeting mummies and griffins and gargoyles and unicorns and saints who came to life in the darkness.

When the subway doors opened Echo walked out fast and that was when she ran into the man. He took her shoulders in his hands and looked into her face. She thought she knew him. But, then, she had just spent a night with the angels in the Metropolitan Museum of Art and fallen asleep on the train home. She could still be dreaming.

He said her name.

If Death is your lover you don't have to be afraid that he will ever leave you. Echo took Mister Bones' hand and started to walk away. What if this man wasn't real? If he would go away again. It had been too long. She had just, after all these years, started to learn that love was not about one boy on a beach pulling you from the waves. It wasn't about one person at all. Was it?

"Echo," he said again.

He followed her up the stairs into the light. She did not look back at him until she was on the sidewalk in the wash of golden blue morning before the heavy cloying heat had started to settle. Now, if I look at him, she told herself, now, in the light, it will be real.

She turned and saw his curls, the sun glinting on the lenses of his glasses. She had painted him so many times like this. But now he looked dusty and tired. His back was slightly hunched. He wasn't a boy anymore.

How? Echo asked. She didn't say it out loud.

"A friend of mine met your Valentine. I was on my way to your home just now."

"Valentine?"

Echo thought of the man Valentine had told her about. He had been waiting at the motel. He had just wanted to massage Valentine's back all night. Valentine said to Echo, "I know it sounds crazy but you of all people would understand. His eyes weren't human. I don't know how else to describe it. He smelled like crushed lavender and mint. He took my sleeping pills but I haven't needed them since."

Echo was dizzy. The sun, reflected in his glasses, hid the eyes of the man from the subway. She gripped onto a traffic-light post. Someone's shopping bag hit against her thigh. The man moved closer, as if to shelter her.

"She's much better now." He took off his glasses and wiped away a layer of sweat and grime. He squinted at Echo. She smelled blueberries. She hadn't bought any yet.

This man who had rescued her from the ocean. But

what about when she was with Thorn, Skye, Smoke? Even Valentine? What about when her father died? He watched her twist the plastic dove ring on her finger.

It was wrong. I wanted you for myself. But it wasn't time yet.

She was shaking. He walked with her. She was trying not to cry. Maybe they had all been her angels, in a way. Delivering her to the next place. Maybe any love we ever have is an angel in whatever form—a little girl fighting death, a white horse who could have been a father once, a boy on the beach.

Echo stopped at the first market and bought some fruit and muffins. Then she was in front of her apartment building. Someone had hosed down the pavement and the heat was already making it steam. She smelled blueberries—had she bought blueberries?—and the Pacific Ocean at night. It smelled like her childhood. It was like before anyone left, anyone got sick, anyone died. She looked up at her window and thought she saw her grandmother Rose's wedding dress stir like a ghost.

"Why didn't you come to me before?" she asked him. "Why did it take you so long?"

He bent his head against his chest. He looked as if his back ached. His eyes were pleading. *It wasn't the time yet. Now it's time.*

She reached for him, touched his warm back.

Then she reached up inside his T-shirt and felt them. They tickled her hands. They were matted, damp with sweat. He looked up at her, looked into her eyes, and nodded.

Echo, on the streets of Manhattan where anything can happen if you believe in it enough. Just like anything can happen in the canyons and underground clubs of Los Angeles if you believe. For magic is belief. Her father had believed in her mother. Her mother believed in the white horse. It had taken Echo this long to believe in Echo and that this man could love her enough.

She tugged gently. The flossy feathers pulled away in her hands like cotton candy, the shabby wings disintegrating, falling from his shoulders, leaving his back bony and naked and so warm in her hands.

In Echo's apartment, Rose's wedding dress was filled with light. It looked alive. Echo lay on the bed and the man took her in his arms.

Then Storm gave Echo back her tears, the ones she had given him so long ago, gave them back deep into her womb, where they would become a child who would never doubt. Who would know that magic is belief and who would believe.

And here I am poised above with my arms spread flying and there are halos of light spinning out of us and yes this is me becoming holy human and my own self.

THE ROSE AND THE BEAST
Fairy Tales Retold

Snow

Tiny

Glass

Charm

Wolf

Rose

Bones

Beast

Ice

Snow

WHEN SHE WAS BORN HER MOTHER WAS SO young, still a girl herself, didn't know what to do with her. She screamed and screamed—the child. Her mother sat crying in the garden. The gardener came by to dig up the soil. It was winter. The child was frost-colored. The gardener stood before the cold winter sun, blocking the light with his broad shoulders. The mother looked like a broken rose bush.

Take her please, the mother cried. The gardener sat beside her. She was shaking. The child would not stop screaming. When the mother put her in his arms, the child was quiet.

Take her, the mother said. I can't keep her. She will

devour me.

The child wrapped her tiny fingers around the gardener's large brown thumb. She stared up at him with her eyes like black rose petals in her snowy face. He said to the mother, Are you sure? And she stood up and ran into the house, sobbing. Are you sure are you sure? She was sure. Take it away, she prayed, it will devour me.

The gardener wrapped the child in a clean towel and put her in his truck and drove her west to the canyon. There was no way he could keep her himself, was there? (He imagined her growing up, long and slim, those lips and eyes.) No, but he knew who could.

The seven brothers lived in a house they had built themselves, built deep into the side of the canyon among the trees. They had built it without chopping down one tree, so it was an odd-shaped house with towers and twisting hallways and jagged staircases. It looked like part of the canyon itself, as if it had sprung up there. It smelled of woodsmoke and leaves. From the highest point you could see the sea lilting and shining in the distance.

This was where the gardener brought the child. He knew these men from work they had all done together on a house by the ocean. He was fascinated by the way they worked. They made the gardener feel slow and awkward and much too tall. Also, lonely.

Bear answered the door. Like all the brothers he had a fine, handsome face, burnished skin, huge brown eyes that regarded everyone as if they were the beloved. He was slightly heavier than the others and his hair was soft, thick, close cropped. He shook the gardener's hand and welcomed him inside, politely avoiding the bundle in the gardener's arms until the gardener said, I don't know where to take her.

Bear brought him into the kitchen where Fox, Tiger, and Buck were eating their lunch of vegetable stew and rice, baked apples and blueberry gingerbread. They asked the gardener to join them. When Bear told them why he was there, they allowed themselves to turn their benevolent gazes to the child in his arms. She stared back at them and the gardener heard an unmistakable burbling coo coming from her mouth.

Buck held her in his muscular arms. She nestled

against him and closed her eyes—dark lash tassels. Buck looked down his fine, sculpted nose at her and whispered, Where does she come from?

The gardener told him, From the valley, her mother can't take care of her. He said he was afraid she would be hurt if he left her there. The mother wasn't well. The brothers gathered around. They knew then that she was the love they had been seeking in every face forever before this. Bear said, We will keep her. And the gardener knew he had done the right thing bringing her here.

The other brothers, Otter, Lynx, and Ram, came home that evening. They also loved her right away, as if they had been waiting forever for her to come. They named her Snow and gave her everything they had.

Bear and Ram built her a room among the trees overlooking the sea. Tiger built her a music-box cradle that rocked and played melodies. Buck sewed her lace dresses and made her tiny boots like the ones he and his brothers wore. They cooked for her—the finest, the healthiest foods, most of which they grew themselves, and she was always surrounded by the flowers Lynx picked from their garden, the candles Fox dipped in the cellar, and the melon-scented soaps that Otter made in his workroom.

She grew up there in the canyon—the only Snow. It was warm in the canyon most days—sometimes winds and rains but never whiteness on the ground. She was their Snow, unbearably white and crystal sweet. She began to grow into a woman and although sometimes this worried them a bit—they were not used to women, especially one like this who was their daughter and yet not—they learned not to be afraid, how to show her as much love as they had when she was a baby and yet give her a distance that was necessary for them as well as for her. As they had given her everything, she gave to them—she learned to hammer and build, cook, sew, and garden. She could do anything. They had given her something else, too—the belief in herself, instilled by seven fathers who had had to learn it. Sometimes at night, gathered around the long wooden table finishing the peach-spice or apple-ginger pies and raspberry tea, they would tell stories of their youth—the things they had suffered separately when they went out alone to try the world. The stories were of freak shows and loneliness and too much liquor or powders and the shame of deformity. They wanted her to know what they had suffered but not to be afraid of it, they wanted her to have everything—the world, too. And to be able to return to them, to safety, whenever she needed. They knew, though, she would not suffer as they had suffered. She was perfect. They were scarred.

She loved them. That is what no one tells. She loved them. They smelled of woodsmoke and sweet earth, where flowers grow. They spoke softly, kindly, sometimes they sang. They were strong and browned from the sun. She believed that they knew everything, could make anything. They loved her as their daughter, sister, mother . . . they loved her. That maybe has been hinted at before, but not that she loved them.

When she was of a certain age the gardener came to visit. He had been reminded of her. The white petals scattering in the garden . . . something, something reminded him, and he came to see what had become of her, if he had been right when he saw her baby face and imagined it grown, and knew he could not keep her.

Lynx looked at him and his eyes were guarded, Lynx's eyes. He did not want to let the gardener in. But he knew, too, this was wrong. The time had come, as they all had known it would. She was a woman now, and restless, and no, they were not her fathers. It was time. So he let the gardener into the house, where she was sitting surrounded by the six other brothers, reading aloud to them. She was wearing a white dress she had made herself, almost as white as her skin, which showed here and there beneath it, and heavy black hobnailed boots like the ones the brothers wore. Her face was flushed and her eyes burned with firelight. The gardener wondered, why had he come here?

She smiled up at him. He was the first man she'd seen, they kept her so sheltered. The first man that was not one of them—a much taller man with a head more like hers. But he did not have their eyes or their strong and lyrical hands.

The gardener was invited to share in the cherry-mint pie she had made for the evening, and he spoke with her, asked about the books she liked to read (they brought her children's stories of magic, and old novels with thick, yellowish pages about passionate women in brutal landscapes) and the music she listened to, did she sew her own dress? She showed him through the night garden she had planted and he knew all about the different bulbs and shrubs, and she liked the way he towered over her and the way his shoulders blocked the moonlight.

The brothers were inside the house trying not to spy, trying to be calm. What could they do? It is time, they told each other.

The gardener left and went back to the woman with whom he had been living all these years. The woman who was Snow's mother. Why had he gone where he had? He could hardly look at her. Why had he gone? He had been right about what that baby would become. Snow's mother was crying when he came home, something was wrong, she could tell it, she could see in his eyes. Something had died.

No, he thought, something has been born.

Something had died.

Snow turned over and over in her bed, her fingers exploring the palpitations of her body under the nightdress. She closed her eyes and saw the gardener's dark curls and tall body. But when she dreamed of him, it was a nightmare. He was cutting down trees with an ax and blood ran from their trunks. He was carrying the body of a very pale child into the woods and holding the ax . . .

They tried to console her, seven brothers, as seven fathers would. They tried to be fair; how could they keep her from living her life? Who were they to keep her? They told her that if he came again she could see him but that they didn't want her to be hurt. Maybe there was another man they could find. She didn't know why, but he was the only one—she wanted to speak to him again. Maybe she could sense her mother on his skin. Her mother. She hardly ever asked about this. She assumed she had been lost and they had found her and there was no one. She was her own mother. But oh something else. Breast. Flowers. Silk. Hair. Lavender. Milk. Apple. Blood. Lost.

The woman who was Snow's mother followed the gardener into the canyon one night. She had grown sick with premonitions. She walked around outside the house in the dark, her feet sinking into the damp earth, the crackle of branches, the smell of crushed flowers. Maybe she was looking for what she had lost too. She thought it was the man, but it was more.

Through the window she saw them, the girl and the gardener. The girl was nightmare. Young young young. Silver white. Perfect. Untorn. Perfect.

The gardener was haloed by her light. Dripping her light. After all, she was the baby he had rescued, she might be dead by now if it weren't for him. After all, she was the same flesh as the woman he had made love to for these years. After all, she was young, perfect, untouched. And he had to rescue her from these seven strange, deformed (suddenly he saw them as deformed) men who would suffocate her, make her a freak like they were.

Poison, the mother thought, poison.

And she came back there when the men were away at work, came back with the apples injected with poison. She had read about it—simple recipe—too messy with razor blades. She had thought of using it on herself in the past. Wouldn't this almost be the same thing?

Snow opened the door and love filled her. She had never seen a woman before. A woman with pale skin and dark hair like hers. Even the redness of the lips and the way the incisors pointed slightly. Something was so familiar that she swooned with it. She had been told not to let strangers in, but this was not a stranger, this was someone she sensed deep in her bones. Like marrow.

The woman said she had brought her a present. Why a present? Your beauty is famous, the woman said. I wanted to honor it. I wanted to see you, too. Some people say we resemble each other.

Snow had never thought of herself as beautiful. For her, beauty was Bear's voice telling her bedtime stories and the way Buck's eyes shone and Lynx's small graceful body. She thought it was strange that this woman would want to give her a present because of how she looked.

The brothers had told her not to accept gifts from strangers, but this wasn't a stranger. This was a woman who seemed so familiar. And the apples were so luscious red sleek. They would be hard clean white fresh inside, chilling and sparking her mouth.

Snow asked if the woman would like to come in? No no she had to be on her way. She was glad to have seen Snow's face.

The woman hesitated for a moment before she left. She looked sad, Snow thought, or worse—but she wasn't sure what it was, and then the woman was leaving.

Snow went inside and washed the apples and began to cut them up for a pie she would give to the brothers. She felt excited—her heart was pounding and, strangely, she wanted to sing. She hummed the lullaby that her music-box cradle had played when she was a baby, rocking by the fireside while the brothers read aloud or talked softly to her.

A woman had come to her door. There were women out there, in the world. How many of them looked like this one? So like her. They couldn't mostly, could they? Who was this woman? Why had she come? Why did she seem sad and her teeth were sharp. Snow imagined them puncturing the sealed sweet red of the apple skin. She reached down and fingered a slice between her thumb and pointer. The skin was dark dark red like blood. Snow put the piece to her lips and ran her tongue along the ridge. She bit.

They found her lying on the floor with the poison in

her veins and the apples spilled where they had rolled. She was the green color of certain white flowers. Each of them tried to expel the poison from her, to breathe life into her. She had a pulse, but hardly—very shallow. They carried her upstairs to the glass bed they had made for her when she outgrew the cradle. When they laid her out in her white dress they wept because without her they knew they would have nothing and their own deaths would come knocking on the door. Seven truncated deaths in fourteen big boots.

My darling, they thought. Sometimes they could not tell if they were having an individual thought or sensing each other's. My darling, we never deserved you. Wake up and we will let you go into the world where you belong. This was our fault, we were wrong to keep you like this. Don't blame us, though. Look at our lives before you. Look at what you gave us.

They called the gardener.

When the gardener came they let him go to her alone. They sat downstairs in the dim—just a single candle—working on the gifts they would give to her if only she woke. These gifts she would take into the world—dresses of silk, necklaces of glass beads and shells, glass candlesticks and champagne glasses and tiny glass animals, candles and incense and bath salts and soaps and quilts and coverlets and a miniature house with a real garden and tiny fountains that she could keep at her bedside.

The gardener went to her and held her hand. It felt like it would slip away, it was so thin and light; it felt boneless. The gardener said he was going to take her away with him, help her get better. Why was he hesitating? He wanted to look at her like this, for a while. He wanted this stillness. She was completely his, now, in a way she would never be again. His silent, perfect bride. Not like the woman who had come screaming to him—what have I done? He brushed the dark, damp strands of hair off her smooth forehead. He leaned close to her, breathing her like one would inhale a bouquet. He looked at her lips, half parted as if waiting for him. He wanted to possess.

But when he touched her with his mouth and her eyes opened she did not see him there. She called for the men, the seven brothers. She wanted them. More than gardeners or mothers. She wanted them the way she needed the earth and the flowers and the sky and the sea from her tower room and food and sleep and warmth and light and nights by the fire and poetry and the stories of going out into the world and almost being destroyed by it and returning to find comfort and the real meaning of freak. And I am a freak, she thought, happily. I am meant to stay here forever. I am loved.

She pushed the gardener away and called for them. In her sleep she had seen love. It was poisoning. It was possessing. Devouring. Or it was seven pairs of boots climbing up the stairs to find her.

Tiny

THE WOMAN NAMED HER LOST BABIES BERRY, Ivy, Oxygen, Pie, Whistler, Willow, Wish, and Pear, never knowing if they were boys or girls. Each one taught her something about life. Sorrow, Pain, Fortitude, Tenderness, Patience, Courage, Awe, Love. She made eight tiny symbolic graves in her garden and planted flowers on them all.

The woman sat alone in her garden of memory flowers, rocking a cradle full of iris bulbs, whispering to babies who could not hear her. She felt like the ancient cracking husk of a pomegranate, rattling with dried seeds.

And then she found she was pregnant again.

The doctors were amazed because the fetus was much too small, but this time there was a perfectly

normal heartbeat flickering on the screen like a miniature star.

The woman prayed to the spirits of the lost babies
that this one would come out all right.

And it did. Except that the baby was tiny, just
about the size of a thumb. Her mother called her
Tiny. You are perfect, the mother told her, the baby I
always wanted. She was careful to make sure her child
did not feel sad because of her small size.

Tiny had to sleep in a cradle made from half a walnut shell and drink out of a thimble. Even dollhouse
doll clothes were too big for her, so mostly she ran
around naked or clothed in scraps of silk.

Tiny didn't know there was anything wrong with
her for a long time. She loved her mother and thought
all mothers were big like that. She believed that when
she was older she might suddenly grow and one day
have a child the size of her own thumb. Her life was
happy. She sat on the edge of the flower box filled with
red, white, and magenta impatiens and watched the
garden bloom. She could see the most infinitesimal
movements of the plants as they grew. It was enough to

occupy her all day, that and being with her mother. She could gaze at her mother forever as if her mother were a lush and flowering plant towering above all the rest.

Tiny was protected from the outside world in the gated garden full of roses, irises, and azaleas, orange, lemon, and avocado trees, and she didn't mind. The garden got more radiant and abundant and redolent every day that she watched it and, as her mother said, blessed it, although she didn't know how she did that, really. She had so much going on inside her head—so many things to dream about. She had eight imaginary playmates that came to her and taught her things about life. About how sad life is, but also how full of wonder, and about being strong and letting go and believing that things will bloom again. Tiny was fine in her tiny world. But one day she saw the boy.

He had climbed over the garden fence because he had heard that the woman with the long legs and the cat eyes lived in that shady, fragrant home. She didn't come out much anymore, people said. The tragedy of her life. They didn't know about her tiny secret.

Tiny saw the boy wandering around the garden, as

intrigued by the flowers as she was, it seemed. It was true, he'd never seen a garden like this one before. The blossoms were huge and the fragrance was staggering. He felt drunk.

He was tall and thin with a long face and deep-set eyes with heavy brows. He was not particularly good-looking—at least he didn't think so. He felt ungainly tripping on his big feet as if to escape his body—cumbersome. But to Tiny he was wonderful. Full of wonder. Terrifying. He was everything she wanted. She stopped caring about the garden and the eight spirit babies who visited her, and even about her mother. Suddenly she resented her mother a little, without quite recognizing the emotion since it was so new to her, but felt it because she realized in that instant that she would never be tall and big like that; she was a freak, she knew, and this boy would never love her.

The boy prowled around the garden, dizzy with the flowers. He was a poet and was already thinking of words to try to describe what he saw (he couldn't). He peeked into the windows of the house and saw the woman walking around with her hair up in a turban towel. She was about his mother's age but she had long legs, high cheekbones, and the upward-slanting sun-flecked green eyes of a cat.

Tiny saw him watching. She needed to scream but she just lay there, oozing and broken like a squashed insect.

The boy waited while Tiny's mother loosened the towel from her head so that her long wet hair shook down. He waited while she let her robe slip from her shoulders. Tiny came closer to him. She could hear his breathing, raspy and deep in his throat, and she could smell something that was better than all the flowers in her garden.

The boy suddenly swung around, sensing, but not seeing anyone. He ran out of the garden.

Tiny thought about him every day and night. She became sullen and would hardly speak or eat. Her mother asked her again and again what was wrong but she wouldn't say. Her eyes became like slits and she chewed on her lips until they bled. She felt like the dead butterfly she had seen moldering in the dirt.

Tiny knew it was time to leave and so she packed up some berries, her bed linens, her thimble, and a sil-

ver needle in a knapsack and began her journey away
from the garden and from the mother whom she would
never be.

If you were Tiny's size you would find that a few
blocks can take a long long time to traverse. There were
many dangers. The bird that swooped down and tried
to eat her for lunch. The toad that fell in love with her
and tried to carry her away to be its wife. The cat that
thought she was a toy to bat around in its claws. With
her silver needle and her quick little body, Tiny was able
to get away. She was no longer a slow dreamer watching the flowers grow. She was a warrior now. Warriors
need something to fight for, though, besides their lives,
because otherwise their lives will not be worth it. Tiny
thought she was fighting for the boy's love, but after a
while she wondered what that meant and how did she
think she could ever achieve it? Small as she was—the
size of one of his fingers—nothing like her mother,
with nothing to give except a way to watch gardens,
some knowledge imparted by eight spirit babies, now
gone, and deftness with a silver needle.

The boy was walking home from school trying to find words to describe the way he was feeling. Alone, awkward, alienated, isolated, crazy. He hated all those words. He wondered why he considered himself a poet. Pretentious as hell. He thought everything he wrote was terrible, actually. He had tried to write about the garden, and the woman in the window, and the strange feeling he had had, as if he were being watched, breathed upon by something that chilled his nape and made him want to cry.

Tiny found him that day. She was half starved. She had been scratched and bitten. Her dress was in tatters. Not one night had she slept well—there was no safe garden, no walnut cradle, no lullaby mother. She was too old for these things anyway, she told herself. Tinys do not deserve safety. If they are to prove themselves, they must suffer and die or suffer and survive.

But then she saw the boy, and love seeped into her body as if she had sucked it from a honeysuckle blossom. She knew he was trying to make up poems. She knew so much about him already. She realized that she was nothing without his desire for poetry, just as she was nothing without her mother's desire for a child. She was their creation; no wonder she had to have them.

This made her feel strangely brave and she leaped as far as she could, landing precariously on his arm. His jacket smelled of smoke and basketball and libraries and the grass he had rolled in, trying to recall what it was like when he was a little boy and not so . . . whatever it was that he was all the time. Sad, depressed, angst-ridden. He didn't even have the right words left for anything.

Tiny jumped from his scratchy sleeve into his pocket, where it was warm and musty smelling. There was a pack of cigarettes, a gnawed pencil stub, some grains of sand, a piece of spearmint gum in case he ever met who he was waiting for. She explored, discovering new things about him. How he worried about lung cancer but couldn't stop smoking. How he always lay on the beach in his clothes, wishing the ocean would take him away, he didn't care where. How he was waiting for his muse, his poetry in the shape of a girl.

And so Tiny waited also, and when he came to his apartment building and went inside, and closed the door of his room that was piled with books replacing tables and chairs and had black-and-white posters from Italian movies on the walls (all the women were so big like Tiny's mother), and had a rumpled bed with sheets like maps—that was when she climbed out of his pocket and stood in front of him. Now she was truly a warrior because he was a million times more dangerous to her than toads, cats, or birds.

Oh, shit, he said. What the fuck.

I'm Tiny, she said.

You can say that again.

I'm Tiny.

He laughed. Man! he said. You are awe-inspiring, O Muse.

I've been trying to find you, she said.

Well, Tiny Muse, I'm certainly glad that you have.

He got down on his knees before her—she was perched on a stack of books of Beat poetry—and stared at every part of her perfect little body. He felt a bit perverse about it, but he didn't care because she seemed to be enjoying his gaze. He knew that he would never be without the right words again as long as she was with him, but he thought he should officially ask her anyway.

Will you help me to find the words, O Muse? he asked.

She looked him up and down, looked around the room.

Can I sleep in your bed? she answered.

He grinned at her and reached for the piece of gum in his pocket.

Suddenly he was translucent, perfect, the size she was.

The prince of the flowers.

Glass

SHE DID NOT MIND HER DAYS ALONE, AWAY from the eyes outside. It was better this way, her secret stories hidden so no one could touch them, take them. Her sisters listened, rapt, but did not try to take. They cared more for the eyes and ears; they seemed to want to collect these like charms to wear around their necks, the eyes and ears and the mouths whispering—beautiful, beautiful, why did it matter she wondered. She was free, still, like a child, the way it is before you are seen and then after that you can never remember who you are unless someone else shows it to you. She had the stories she gave to her sisters that made them love her. Or need her, at least.

And she had the tasks. She loved to plant the beds with lilies and wisteria, camellias and gardenias, until her hands were caked with earth. To arrange the flowers in the vase like dancing sisters. To make the salmon in pomegranate sauce; the salads of spinach, red onion, pine nuts, oranges, and avocados; the golden vanilla cream custards; the breads and piecrusts that powdered her with flour. She loved, even, to dust the things, to feel them in her hands, imagining their history. The glass music box that perhaps a boy had once given to his grandparents—the first present he had ever chosen, making them close their eyes, watching them standing there, before him, suddenly looking so small with their eyelids closed and their hands held out until they heard the tinkle of their first dance. The glass goblet with the roses and grape clusters one could feel with the fingertips like Braille that perhaps a man had given to his wife because she was losing her sight and he was afraid to give her more books of poetry. The candlesticks like crystal balls, many-faceted; though the girl could not read her own future in them perhaps if she looked closely enough she could see the young bride tearing away the tissue and holding them up to the light to see herself being imagined by this girl, now. This girl, now, who did not mind polishing the wooden floors or scrubbing out the pots until her sisters could see their reflections, or cleaning between the tiles and lighting the candles, running the water and scattering the petals and powders in the bath so that her sisters could lie in the tub where she would tell them stories. Always she would tell them stories; they returned at night and sat before their mirrors, let her rub their feet with almond oil, soothe them with her words and in this way she felt loved.

But the woman came to her then. The woman with hair of red like roses, hair of white like snowfall. She was young and old. She was blind and could see everything. She spoke softly, in whispers, but her voice carried across the mountain ranges like sleeping giants, the cities lit like fairies and the oceans—undulating mermaids. She laughed at her own sorrow and wept pearls at weddings. Her fingers were branches and her eyes were little blue planets. She said, You cannot hide forever, though you may try. I've seen you in the kitchen, in the garden. I've seen the things you have sewn—curtains of dawn, twilight blankets and dresses for the sisters like a garden of stars. I have heard the stories you tell. You are the one who transforms, who creates. You can go out into the world and show others. They will feel less alone because of you, they will feel understood, unburdened by you, awakened by you, freed of guilt and shame and sorrow. But to share with them you must wear shoes you must go out you must not hide you must dance and it will be harder you must face jealousy and sometimes rage and desire and love which can hurt most of all because of what can then be taken away. So make that astral dress to fit your own body this time. And here are glass shoes made from your words, the stories you have told like a blower with her torch forming the thinnest, most translucent sheets of light out of what was once sand. But be careful; sand is already broken but glass breaks. The shoes are for dancing not for running away.

So she washed off the dust and ash and flour and mud and went to the dance where sure enough everyone whirled around her, entranced by the stories in which they recognized themselves, but in the stories they were also more than themselves and it always felt at the end

fulfilled not meaningless and empty like life can sometimes feel. She knew they all loved her with her stories
because they became her and she became them.

He came to her across the marble floor, past the tall
windows glowing like candles, the balconies overlooking the reflecting pools full of swans, the stone statues
of goddesses and beds of heady roses—had she made
all of this, like a story? He had dense curls and soft
full lips and bright eyes like a woodland beast and a
body of lithe muscle and mostly she could see he was
gentle, he was gentle like a boy though he could lift her
in his hands. He held her and she felt his hard chest
and stomach and hipbones and she felt his strong heart
beating like the sound of all the stories she could ever
hope to tell. Maybe she had not created him, maybe she
was his creation and all she dreamed, his dream. Or
maybe they had made each other. Yes.

Beloved. One. He planted in her a seed of a white
flower with a dizzy scent; in the night garden the
oranges hung like fat moonstruck jewels and the jasmine bloomed as she spun and spun. Now she had everything and the sisters eyed her jealously, secretly, in

their mirrors until the glass cracked, clutched the little bags she had made for them until the crystal beads scattered and broke—they had stories, too, they'd like to tell. They'd like to make someone cry and swoon and spin with love for what they made. Who was she to take this away from them? How dare she wear the glass shoes? They could see what was wrong with her. She wasn't perfect, she wasn't so beautiful. Her skin was blemished and her body was too thin, or not thin enough, and she wasn't perfectly symmetrical and her hair was thin and brittle and why was he looking at her like that? It was just that she knew how to make things. Or not even that—just rearrange, imitate.

She felt their envy and this broke her. The story ended, she couldn't tell the rest, they'd hate her, she had to stop it, she wasn't any good shut up you bad bad girl ugly and you don't deserve any of this and so the spell was broken and she ran home through a tangle of words where the letters jumbled and made no sense and meant nothing, and the words were ugly and she was not to be heard or seen, she was blemished and too fat, too thin, not smart, too smart, not good, not a storyteller, not a creator, not beautiful, not a woman not not not. All the things that girls feel they are not when they fear that if they become, if they are, they will no longer be loved by the sisters whose hearts they have not meant to break. And besides, if the sisters are gone and only the beloved remains with his dense curls and his lips, how safe are you then? You have to have him or you will die if the sisters are gone with their listening ears and their feet to rub and their bodies to dress and their shared loneliness.

She lost one of the glass slippers—shine, fire, bright of her making like a dropped word lost, like a word, the missing word to make the story right again, to make it complete.

It doesn't matter, she tells herself, shredding up the dress she made. It doesn't matter, I am safe. Alone and safe. The sisters don't hate me. I am small and safe, no one will hate me, hear me, no one can break me by leaving, by taking away his seed, the promise of the jasmine blossom in the garden.

Still he came to find her even without her enchantments, her stories, her dress, her shoe. He had the shoe, he'd found it when he followed her. It was so fragile he didn't breathe.

She made him want to cry when he walked up the path through the ferns and doves and lilies and saw her covered with earth and dust and ash. Only her eyes shone out. Revealing, not reflecting. Windows. Her feet were bare. He wanted her to tell him the rest of the story. He felt bereft without it, without her. There were only these women with mirror eyes strutting across marble floors, tossing their manes, revealing their breasts, untouchable, only these tantalizing empty glass boxes full of dancing lights he could not hold, only these icy cubicles, parched yards, hard loneliness.

When the sisters saw him kneeling before her holding the one shoe, not breathing, trying not to crush anything, saw how he looked at her, how he needed her, they knew that if they tried to take this from her they would never know, have nothing left, they would starve, they would break, they would never wake up.

The fairy who was not old, not young, who was red roses, white snowfall, who was blind and saw everything, who sent stories resounding through the universe

said, You must reach inside yourselves where I live like
a story, not old, not young, laughing at my own sorrow,
weeping pearls at weddings, wielding a torch to melt
sand into something clear and bright.

Charm

SHE FELT LIKE THE GIRL IN THE FAIRY TALE.
Maybe there had been some kind of curse. Inevitable
that she would prick her arm (not her finger) with the
needle. Did the girl feel this ecstasy of pure honeyed
light in her veins, like being infused with the soul she
had lost? For Rev, that was all there was.

The flood was like an ogre's tears. Mud and trees
and even small children were carried away in it. Rev's
vintage Thunderbird was swept down the canyon,
landing crashed at the bottom, full of water and leaves.

Fires like dragon's breath consumed the poppies and
lupine, the jacaranda trees that once flowered purple in
sudden overnight bursts of exuberance as if startled at
their own capacity for gorgeousness.

When the earth quaked, the walls of Rev's house

cracked; all the glasses and teacups in her cabinet careened out, covering the floor in a sharp carpet that cut her feet as she ran outside. Chimneys and windows wailed. Rev was amazed at how, with the power all out, she could see the stars above her, clearly, for the first time since she was a child on a camping trip in the desert. They were like the glass fragments on the floor. The air smelled of leaking gas. Her feet were bleeding into the damp lawn.

This is my city, Rev thought. Cursed, like I am cursed. Sleeping, like I sleep. Tear-flooded and fever-scorched, quaking and bloodied with nightmares.

She went out in the city with its lights like a radio-active phosphorescence, wandered through galleries where the high-priced art on the walls was the same as the graffiti scrawled outside by taggers who were arrested or killed for it, went to parties in hotel rooms where white-skinned, lingerie-clad rock stars had been staying the night their husbands shot themselves in the head, listened to music in nightclubs where stunning boyish actors had OD'd on the pavement. When the sun began to come up Rev went back to her canyon house where vines had begun to grow through the cracks in the walls. The air smelled acrid and stale—eucalyptus and cigarettes. Her television was always on.

Pop came by in his dark glasses, leather pants, and long blond dreadlocks. He gave her what she needed in a needle in exchange for the photos he took of her. And sometimes she slept with him.

Sleeping Beauty, he said. I like you this way.

She was wearing her kimono with the embroidered red roses, her hair in her face. Hipbones haunting through silk and flesh.

You have opium eyes.

Opium eyes. She closed her heavy lids over them, wanting to sleep.

He photographed her as witch, priestess, fairy queen, garden. He photographed her at the ruins of the castle and on the peeling, mournful carousel and in the fountain.

It's like you're from nowhere, Pop said. I like that. It's like you live inside my head. I made you just the way I wanted you to be.

Where am I from? she wondered. Maybe Pop was

right. She was only in his head. But there had been something before.

She had been adopted by a man and a woman who wanted beauty. The woman thought of champagne roses, rose champagne, perfume, and jewels, but she couldn't have a child. The child they found was darker than they had hoped for but even more lavishly numinous. They had men take pictures of her right from the beginning. There were things that happened. Rev tried to think only of the leopard couches and velvet pillows, the feather boas and fox fur pelts, the flock of doves and the poodle with its forelock twisted into a unicorn horn, the hot lights that were, she hoped, bright enough to sear away the image of what was happening to her. She could not, though she tried, remember the face of the other girl who had been there once.

Was the curse that she was born too beautiful? Had it caused her real parents to abandon her, fearful of the length of lash, the plush of lip in such a young face? Was it the reason the men with cameras had sucked away her soul in little sips, because any form that lovely must remain soulless so as not to stun them impotent?

Was it what made Old-Woman-Heroin's face split into a jealous leer as she beckoned Rev up to the attic and stabbed her with the needle that first time?

Because she no longer had a car, she let Pop drive her around. He picked her up one night and took her to a small white villa. It belonged to an actress named Miss Charm. Pop led Rev upstairs, past the sleek smoky people drinking punch out of an aquarium and into a room that was painted to look like a shell. He told her to take off her dress and arranged her limbs on a big white bed, tied and slapped her arm, tucked the needle into the largest, least bruised vein. Then the three men climbed onto her while Pop hovered around them snapping shots. Rev did not cry out. She lay still. She let the opium be her soul. It was better than having a soul. It did not cry out, it did not writhe with pain.

Get off of her, you fucks! a voice screamed like the soul Rev no longer had.

The young woman had shorn black hair and pale skin.

Get out of my house, she said.

Oh chill, Charm.

Leave now, she said.

Want to join the party? one of the men said. I think she wants to join the party.

Rev felt her empty insides trying to jump out of her as if to prove there was no soul there, nothing anyone had to be afraid of, nothing left for them to want to have. She felt her emptiness bitter and burning coming up from her throat. The other woman held up a small sharp kitchen knife and the men moved away.

The pale woman helped Rev to the bathroom and wiped her face with a warm wet towel. Rev looked at her reflection in the mirror. She had shadows underneath her eyes as if her makeup had been put on upside down. But in spite of that, nothing had changed. She still bore the curse.

You're going to be okay, the woman was saying in a hard voice like: you have to be.

Rev stared at her.

I know, the woman said.

She ran a bath for Rev and lit the candles that were arranged around the tub like torches along the ramparts of a castle. She filled the water with oils that smelled like the bark, leaves, and blossoms of trees from a sacred grove. The mirrors blurred with steam like a mystic fog so that Rev could not see her own image. She was thankful.

While Rev bathed, the woman stripped off the sheets from the white bed and bleached and boiled them clean. She opened all the windows that looked out over the courtyard full of banana trees, Chinese magnolia, bird of paradise, and hibiscus flowers. She lit incense in sconces all around the room and played a tape of Tibetan monks chanting.

Rev got out of the bath and dried herself off with the clean white towel the woman had left for her. She put on the heavy clean white robe that had been stolen from some fancy hotel and walked barefoot into the bedroom.

Are you hungry? the woman asked.

Rev shook her head.

Do you want to sleep here tonight?

Rev nodded. Sleep sleep sleep. That was what she wanted.

She woke the next night. The woman was sitting at her bedside with a silver tray. She had made a meal of jasmine rice, coconut milk, fresh mint, and chiles. There were tall glasses of mineral water with slices of lime like green moons rising above clear bubbling pools. There was a glass bowl full of gardenias.

Can you eat now? There was an expression on the woman's face that seemed vaguely familiar. Rev thought of how her adopted mother's face had looked when she would not get out of bed after something had happened with the photographer. No, it was not that. Maybe she was remembering another woman, before that one. A woman with eyes that were always wet.

I thought I forgot her, Rev said. My real mother. You remind me of her.

How?

Because of your eyes now.

What happened? Why was she crying?

I used to think she gave me up because I was cursed.

Cursed? the woman said.

Rev looked down and pulled the blankets up over her heavy, satiny breasts.

Blessed, said the woman. She was crying because you are blessed and because she had to give you up.

The woman was wearing a white men's T-shirt. Her face was scrubbed clean of makeup. Her cheekbones were almost equine. She had a few freckles over the bridge of her nose. Eat something now, she said.

Rev found, strangely, that she was hungry. She ate the sweet and spicy, creamy minty rice and drank the fizzing lime-stung mineral water. She breathed the gardenias. She watched the woman's eyes. They were like the eyes of old-time movie stars, always lambent, making the celluloid look slicked with water, lit with candles.

You can stay here as long as you need to, the woman said.

But I'm going to need . . . Rev began.

If you need it I'll get it for you. Until you decide you want to stop. I stopped.

Rev nodded. Her hair fell forward over her face.

If you need me I'll be sleeping in the next room, said the woman.

But this is your bed, said Rev.

It's yours for now.

She stroked Rev's hand.

Rev slept for days and days. Sometimes she woke

kicking her legs and feet until the comforter slid from
the bed. Then she would feel someone covering her
with satin and down again, touching her clammy
forehead with dry, soft, gardenia-scented fingertips.
Sometimes she woke shivering, sweating, quaking or
parched. Always the hands would be there to warm or
cool or still her, to hold a shimmering glass of water to
her cracking lips.

Sometimes Rev dreamed she was in a garden gathering flowers that bit at her hands with venemous
mouths. She dreamed she was running from creatures
who bared needles instead of teeth. One of them caught
her and pierced her neck. She was falling falling down
a spiral staircase into darkness. She was lying in a cof-
fin that was a castle, suffocating under roses. A woman
came and knelt beside her, to stitch up her wounds with
a silver needle and golden thread.

One night Rev heard, through the mother-of-pearl-
painted walls, the soft, muffled animal sounds of someone crying. She got out of bed like a sleepwalker. The
night was warm and soft on her bare skin. It clothed
her like the robe the princess had dreamed of spinning

when she found the old woman in the attic—a fabric
of gold filigree lace. How many years the princess had
dreamed of spinning such a garment. But there were
never any spinning wheels to be found in the whole
kingdom. And then, finally, when her chance had come
to ornament her beauty the way she wished, for the
imagined forbidden lover with the small high breasts
and sweet, wet hair and gentle eyes, she had pricked
herself and fallen into the death sleep.

Perhaps it was what she deserved for wanting to
make herself more beautiful. And for wanting what
she could not have.

Rev went out the bedroom door and into the hall.
The house was dark and silent except for the sound of
muffled weeping.

In the room where the woman lay it was darker
still. Rev found her way to the bed by sound and touch.
Her hands caught onto something warm and curved
and fragile-feeling. It was the woman's hipbone jutting
out from beneath the blankets.

Why are you crying? Rev asked. Her hand slid
down over the hipbone, across the woman's taut

abdomen working with sobs.

The woman reached for a silk tassel and pulled the embroidered piano-shawl curtains back. Moonlight flooded the room. She handed Rev a small battered black-and-white photograph.

Do you remember? the woman asked.

Rev stared at the two naked young girls, one dark, one pale, curled on a leopard-skin sofa. Their hands and feet were shackled together. It was herself and the woman. That was why the eyes had looked familiar.

My stepfather took this, the woman said.

These two girls. Only with each other were they young. They would take each other's hands and run screaming through the night. No one could touch them, then. Dressed as ragged, raging boys; people were afraid of them. Devouring stolen roses and gardenias, stuffing their faces with petals. Rolling in the dirt, scratching so that their nails ached, filled with soil. The fair-skinned one would bind the other's breasts, gently, gently, so they were hidden away in the flannel shirt. The dark-skinned one would wipe the powder and paint from the other's face. They would trace each other's initials

with a razor blade on their palms and hold hands till
their blood was one. These secret rampages were their
own—they could look at each other anywhere, no matter what was happening around them—to them—and
be free, be back, roaming, hollering, shrieking, untouched except by each other.

Charm, Rev said. Miss Charm.

I shouldn't have asked you to stay, said Charm. I
shouldn't have made you remember.

I'll go then, Rev said. If you want.

I don't want you to go, Charm whispered. I've been
waiting for you so long. Her voice reminded Rev of a
piece of broken jewelry.

I thought he had taken my soul, said Rev.

I thought he took mine, too. But no one can. It's just
been sleeping.

When Charm kissed her, Rev felt as if all the fierce
blossoms were shuddering open. The castle was opening. She felt as if the other woman were breathing into
her body something long lost and almost forgotten. It
was, she knew, the only drug either of them would
need now.

Wolf

THEY DON'T BELIEVE ME. THEY THINK I'M CRAZY. But let me tell you something it be a wicked wicked world out there if you didn't already know.

My mom and he were fighting and that was nothing new. And he was drinking, same old thing. But then I heard her mention me, how she knew what he was doing. And no fucking way was she going to sit around and let that happen. She was taking me away and he better not try to stop her. He said, no way, she couldn't leave.

That's when I started getting scared for both of us, my mom and me. How the hell did she know about that? He would think for sure I told her. And then he'd do what he had promised he'd do every night he held me under the crush of his putrid skanky body.

I knew I had to get out of there. I put all my stuff together as quick and quiet as possible—just some clothes, and this one stuffed lamb my mom gave me when I was little and my piggy-bank money that I'd been saving—and I climbed out the window of the condo. It was a hot night and I could smell my own sweat but it was different. I smelled the same old fear I'm used to but it was mixed with the night and the air and the moon and the trees and it was like freedom, that's what I smelled on my skin.

Same old boring boring story America can't stop telling itself. What is this sicko fascination? Every book and movie practically has to have a little, right? But why do you think all those runaways are on the streets tearing up their veins with junk and selling themselves so they can sleep in the gutter? What do you think the alternative was at home?

I booked because I am not a victim by nature. I had been planning on leaving, but I didn't want to lose my mom and I knew the only way I could get her to leave him was if I told her what he did. That was out of the question, not only because of what he might do to me but what it would do to her.

I knew I had to go back and help her, but I have to admit to you that at that moment I was scared shitless and it didn't seem like the time to try any heroics. That's when I knew I had to get to the desert because there was only one person I had in the world besides my mom.

I really love my mom. You know we were like best friends and I didn't even really need any other friend. She was so much fun to hang with. We cut each other's hair and shared clothes. Her taste was kind of young-ish and cute, but it worked because she looked pretty young. People thought we were sisters. She knew all the song lyrics and we sang along in the car. We both can't carry a tune. Couldn't? What else about her? It's so hard to think of things sometimes, when you're try-ing to describe somebody so someone else will know. But that's the thing about it—no one can ever know. Basically you're totally alone and the only person in the world who made me feel not completely that way was her because after all we were made of the same stuff. She used to say to me, Baby, I'll always be with you.

No matter what happens to me I'm still here. I believed
her until he started coming into my room. Maybe she
was still with me but I couldn't be with her those times.
It was like if I did then she'd hurt so bad I'd lose her
forever.

I figured the only place I could go would be to the
desert, so I got together all my money and went to the
bus station and bought a ticket. On the ride I started
getting the shakes real bad thinking that maybe I
shouldn't have left my mom alone like that and maybe
I should go back but I was chickenshit, I guess. I leaned
my head on the glass and it felt cool and when we got
out of the city I started feeling a little better like I could
breathe. L.A. isn't really so bad as people think. I guess.
I mean there are gangs at my school but they aren't really active or violent except for the isolated incident. I
have experienced one big earthquake in my life and it
really didn't bother me so much because I'd rather feel
out of control at the mercy of nature than other ways, if
you know what I mean. I just closed my eyes and let it
ride itself out. I kind of wished he'd been on top of me
then because it might have scared him and made him

feel retribution was at hand, but I seriously doubt that. I don't blame the earth for shaking because she is probably so sick of people fucking with her all the time—building things and poisoning her and that. L.A. is also known for the smog, but my mom said that when she was growing up it was way worse and that they had to have smog alerts all the time where they couldn't do P.E. Now that part I would have liked because P.E. sucks. I'm not very athletic, maybe 'cause I smoke, and I hate getting undressed in front of some of those stupid bitches who like to see what kind of underwear you have on so they can dis you in yet another ingenious way. Anyway, my smoking is way worse for my lungs than the smog, so I don't care about it too much. My mom hated that I smoke and she tried everything—tears and the patch and Nicorette and homeopathic remedies and trips to an acupuncturist, but finally she gave up.

I was wanting a cigarette bad on that bus and thinking about how it would taste, better than the normal taste in my mouth, which I consider tainted by him, and how I can always weirdly breathe a lot better when

I have one. My mom read somewhere that smokers smoke as a way to breathe more, so yoga is supposed to help, but that is one thing she couldn't get me to try. My grandmother, I knew she wouldn't mind the smoking—what could she say? My mom called her Barb the chimney. There is something so dry and brittle, so sort of flammable about her, you'd think it'd be dangerous for her to light up like that.

I liked the desert from when I visited there. I liked that it was hot and clean-feeling, and the sand and rocks and cactus didn't make you think too much about love and if you had it or not. They kind of made your mind still, whereas L.A.—even the best parts, maybe especially the best parts, like flowering trees and neon signs and different kinds of ethnic food and music—made you feel agitated and like you were never really getting what you needed. Maybe L.A. had some untapped resources and hidden treasures that would make me feel full and happy and that I didn't know about yet but I wasn't dying to find them just then. If I had a choice I'd probably like to go to Bali or someplace like that where people are more natural and believe in art and dreams and color and love. Does any place like that exist? The main reason L.A. was okay was because that is where my mom was and anywhere she was I had decided to make my home.

On the bus there was this boy with straight brown hair hanging in his pale freckled face. He looked really sad. I wanted to talk to him so much but of course I didn't. I am freaked that if I get close to a boy he will somehow find out what happened to me—like it's a scar he'll see or a smell or something, a red flag—and he'll hate me and go away. This boy kind of looked like maybe something had happened to him, too, but you can't know for sure. Sometimes I'd think I'd see signs of it in people but then I wondered if I was just trying not to feel so alone. That sounds sick, I guess, trying to almost wish what I went through on someone else for company. But I don't mean it that way. I don't wish it on anyone, believe me, but if they've been there I would like to talk to them about it.

The boy was writing furiously in a notebook, like maybe a journal, which I thought was cool. This journal now is the best thing I've ever done in my whole life. It's the only good thing really that they've given me here.

One of our assignments was to write about your perfect dream day. I wonder what this boy's perfect dream day would be. Probably to get to fuck Pamela Lee or something. Unless he was really as cool as I hoped, in which case it would be to wake up in a bed full of cute kitties and puppies and eat a bowl full of chocolate chip cookies in milk and get on a plane and get to go to a warm, clean, safe place (the cats and dogs would arrive there later, not at all stressed from their journey) where you could swim in blue-crystal water all day naked without being afraid and you could lie in the sun and tell your best friend (who was also there) your funniest stories so that you both laughed so hard you thought you'd pop and at night you got to go to a restaurant full of balloons and candles and stuffed bears, like my birthdays when I was little, and eat mounds of ice cream after removing the circuses of tiny plastic animals from on top.

In my case, the best friend would be my mom, of course, and maybe this boy if he turned out to be real cool and not stupid.

I fell asleep for a little while and I had this really bad dream. I can't remember what it was but I woke up feeling like someone had been slugging me. And then I thought about my mom, I waited to feel her there with me, like I did whenever I was scared, but it was like those times when he came into my room—she wasn't anywhere. She was gone then and I think that was when I knew but I wouldn't let myself.

I think when you are born an angel should say to you, hopefully kindly and not in the fake voice of an airline attendant: Here you go on this long, long dream. Don't even try to wake up. Just let it go on until it is over. You will learn many things. Just relax and observe because there just is pain and that's it mostly and you aren't going to be able to escape no matter what. Eventually it will all be over anyway. Good luck.

I had to get off the bus before the boy with the notebook and as I passed him he looked up. I saw in his journal that he hadn't been writing but sketching, and he ripped out a page and handed it to me. I saw it was a picture of a girl's face but that is all that registered because I was thinking about how my stomach had dropped, how I had to keep walking, step by step, and get off the bus and I'd never be able to see him again and somehow it really really mattered.

When I got off the bus and lit up I saw that the picture was me—except way prettier than I think I look, but just as sad as I feel. And then it was too late to do anything because the bus was gone and so was he.

I stopped at the liquor store and bought a bag of pretzels and a Mountain Dew because I hadn't eaten all day and my stomach was talking pretty loud. Everything tasted of bitter smoke. Then after I'd eaten I started walking along the road to my grandma's. She lives off the highway on this dirt road surrounded by cactus and other desert plants. It was pretty dark so you could see the stars really big and bright, and I thought how cold the sky was and not welcoming or magical at all. It just made me feel really lonely. A bat flew past like a sharp shadow and I could hear owls and coyotes. The coyote howls were the sound I would have made if I could have. Deep and sad but scary enough that no one would mess with me, either.

My grandma has a used stuff store so her house is like

this crazy warehouse full of junk like those little plaster
statuettes from the seventies of these ugly little kids with
stupid sayings that are supposed to be funny, and lots of
old clothes like army jackets and jeans and ladies' nylon
shirts, and cocktail glasses, broken china, old books, trin-
kets, gadgets, just a lot of stuff that you think no one would
want but they do, I guess, because she's been in business
a long time. Mostly people come just to talk to her because she is sort of this wise woman of the desert who's
been through a lot in her life and then they end up buying
something, I think, as a way to pay her back for the free
counseling. She's cool, with a desert-lined face and a ban-
danna over her hair and long skinny legs in jeans. She was
always after my mom to drop that guy and move out here
with her but my mom wouldn't. My mom still was holding on to her secret dream of being an actress but nothing
had panned out yet. She was so pretty, I thought it would,
though. Even though she had started to look a little older.
But she could have gotten those commercials where they
use the women her age to sell household products and as-
pirin and stuff. She would have been good at that because
of her face and her voice, which are kind and honest and

you just trust her.

I hadn't told Grandma anything about him, but I think she knew that he was fucked up. She didn't know how much, though, or she wouldn't have let us stay there. Sometimes I wanted to go and tell her, but I was afraid then Mom would have to know and maybe hate me so much that she'd kick me out.

My mom and I used to get dressed up and put makeup on each other and pretend to do commercials. We had this mother-daughter one that was pretty cool. She said I was a natural, but I wouldn't want to be an actor because I didn't like people looking at me that much. Except that boy on the bus, because his drawing wasn't about the outside of my body, but how I felt inside and you could tell by the way he did it, and the way he smiled, that he understood those feelings so I didn't mind that he saw them. My mom felt that I'd be good anyway, because she said that a lot of actors don't like people looking at them and that is how they create these personas to hide behind so people will see that and the really good ones are created to hide a lot of things. I guess for that reason I might be okay but I still hated the idea of going on auditions and having people tell me I wasn't pretty enough or something. My mom said it was interesting and challenging but I saw it start to wear on her.

Grandma wasn't there when I knocked so I went around the back, where she sat sometimes at night to smoke, and it was quiet there, too. That's when I started feeling sick like at night in my bed trying not to breathe or vomit. Because I saw his Buick sitting there in the sand.

Maybe I have read too many fairy tales. Maybe no one will believe me.

I poked around the house and looked through the windows and after a while I heard their voices and I saw them in this cluttered little storage room piled up with the stuff she sells at the store. Everything looked this glazed brown fluorescent color. When I saw his face I knew something really bad had happened. I remembered the dream I had had and thought about my mom. All of a sudden I was inside that room, I don't really remember how I got there, but I was standing next to my grandma and I saw she had her shotgun in her hand.

He was saying, Barb, calm down, now, okay. Just calm down. When he saw me his eyes narrowed like dark slashes and I heard a coyote out in the night.

My grandmother looked at me and at him and her mouth was this little line stitched up with wrinkles. She kept looking at him but she said to me, Babe, are you okay?

I said I had heard him yelling at mom and I left. She asked him what happened with Nance and he said they had a little argument, that was all, put down the gun, please, Barb.

Then I just lost it, I saw my grandma maybe start to back down a little and I went ballistic. I started screaming how he had raped me for years and I wanted to kill him and if we didn't he'd kill us. Maybe my mom was already dead.

I don't know what else I said, but I do know that he started laughing at me, this hideous tooth laugh, and I remembered him above me in that bed with his clammy hand on my mouth and his ugly ugly weight and me trying to keep hanging on because I wouldn't let him take my mom away, that was the one thing he could never do and now he had. Then I had the gun and I pulled the trigger. My grandma had taught me how once, without my mom knowing, in case I ever needed to defend myself, she said.

My grandma says that she did it. She says that he came at us and she said to him, I've killed a lot prettier, sweeter innocents than you with this shotgun, meaning the animals when she used to go out hunting, which is a pretty good line and everything, but she didn't do it. It was me.

I have no regrets about him. I don't care about much anymore, really. Only one thing.

Maybe one night I'll be asleep and I'll feel a hand like a dove on my cheekbone and feel her breath cool like peppermints and when I open my eyes my mom will be there like an angel, saying in the softest voice, When you are born it is like a long, long dream. Don't try to wake up. Just go along until it is over. Don't be afraid. You may not know it all the time but I am with you. I am with you.

Rose

WHEN ROSE WHITE AND ROSE RED ARE LITTLE,
they tell each other, We will never need anyone else
ever, we are going to do everything together. It doesn't
matter if we never find anyone else. We are complete.

Rose White is smaller and thinner and her hair
is like morning sunlight; it breaks easily. Rose Red is
faster and stronger and her hair is like raging sunset
and could be used to hang jewels around someone's
neck. Rose White is quiet and Rose Red talks fast, she
is always coming up with ideas—they will go ride the
rapids, climb down to the bottom of the canyons, travel
to far-off lands where babies wear nothing but flowers and their feet can never touch the floor. Rose Red's

voice evokes volcanoes, salt spray, cool tunnels of air, hot plains, redolence, blossoms. Rose White listens and smiles. Yes—worlds, waters, rocks, stars, color so much color. She can see it all when Rose Red speaks. She can see herself balanced precariously on steep precipices or swimming through churning waters—with Rose Red.

Rose Red gives Rose White courage and Rose White gives Rose Red peace. Rose White brushes out the fiery tangle of Rose Red's hair, helps her pick out her dresses, makes her sit down to eat her meals. Rose White makes pumkin soup, salads of melon and mints and edible flowers. She makes dresses out of silk scarves. When Rose Red's heart quickens and her skin flushes like her hair, Rose White listens to her until she is quiet, tells her she is right—the world is a strange mad place, it isn't Rose Red who is mad. Rose Red's world is where she wants to live.

When Rose White gets too quiet, too cold, too deep within herself, afraid to speak, afraid to be seen, Rose Red puts a hat on her head, takes her hand, and brings her out where it is warm and bright. Even though they have not traveled far, with Rose Red it is always an adventure. She knows places to go where you can dance to live drums, eat spicy foods with your hands, buy magic talismans.

One day Rose Red takes Rose White farther away than they have been before. They are in the woods gathering berries—which they eat till their hands and tongues are purple—burying their faces in the pine needles, practicing bird calls, chasing butterflies. They climb trees and bathe in a stream and adorn themselves with moss and vines and wildflowers. They lose track of time. Rose Red does because she wants time to be lost and Rose White does because she trusts Rose Red and so forgets to worry. But then it is suddenly night and the trees become hovering specters and the wind is lost ghosts and the owls are mournful phantoms. Rose White is afraid and Rose Red is becoming afraid, not of the night but because she is not sure she can console Rose White this time, or regain her trust. We'll be all right, she says. We have each other. But she knows that, as the night goes on, Rose White is not content with this—she wants to be rescued, she wants someone from the outside who has a light and strength that Rose Red does not have. Rose White is crying and her dress keeps getting caught on branches and her face is scratched and she is cold. Rose Red gives her her sweater but it doesn't help much. Rose White is shivering. She says, How could this have happened? What were we thinking? We've got to get help. This is how girls die. She is sobbing.

Then Rose Red sees the light shining in the trees. To Rose Red the light is like Rose White, it is made for Rose White. Her relief is not for herself—if it wasn't for Rose White, Rose Red would stay out in the forest until dawn, maybe for days and nights, maybe forever, growing wilder and wilder until she is a part of the trees and dirt and darkness—but Rose White is more important to her than all the freedom and all the wildness she desires. She has to raise her voice so that Rose White will stop crying and hear her—There, see the light, there, for you.

They go toward it and when they see the little cottage they are not afraid, even Rose White is not afraid because the cottage is made of round stones with a thatched roof and a smoking chimney and moss growing on the walls and a carefully tended garden. They go up the little stone path among the hollyhocks, morning glories, the carrots and tomatoes and strawberry vines, and Rose Red knocks on the little green door with the big brass knocker.

No one answers. Rose Red peeks through the lace-curtained window. She sees a room warmed by fire-light, a wooden floor, cushions, a small table with a blue-and-white-checked cloth and a milk pitcher full of daisies and honeysuckle. Come on, Rose Red gestures, and she gently pushes the door open.

That is when they see the Bear. Rose White steps back but Rose Red reaches for her hand and they stand very still. The Bear blinks up at them with his flickering fire-lit brown eyes. The tip of his snout quivers. His breathing is labored. He shifts his weight and his front paws sway in the air. His claws are long and sharp. Rose White and Rose Red hold their breath.

He's hurt, Rose Red says. Yes, there is a large wound in the Bear's side. His blood is pooling onto the braid rug. Rose Red moves slowly toward him. It's all right, she says, we won't hurt you. Let me see you.

She kneels down and they look at each other. The

Bear smells of forests, smoke, berries. After a long time, Rose Red moves closer. She puts out her hand, palm down. The Bear sniffs it, licks it with his long, rough, pink tongue. Yes, there, it's all right, Rose Red says.

Rose Red goes and fills a basin with water from the well outside. She gives it to the Bear to drink. Rose White takes some berries from her pockets and holds out her hand. The Bear nuzzles her palm with his damp snout, tickles her as he eats. Rose White rips a piece of cloth from the bottom of her dress. She and Rose Red wash the wound and gently bandage it. The Bear lies back awkwardly, heavily, on the cushions and watches them. That is when Rose White realizes what it is he reminds her of. She can't stop thinking this. She is less surprised by the thought than by the realization that she does not want to share it with the person who has known every single thing about her since the day they were born.

After a while Rose Red and Rose White fall asleep. In the morning they feed the Bear again and help themselves to bread and honey and cheese, milk and berries. They go out into the woods. Neither of them mentions

the idea of going home. They forage for food for the
Bear. Roots, nuts, more berries. A little ways from the
cottage they find a beehive that someone has been tend-
ing, and Rose Red puts on the beekeeper's suit and col-
lects some of the honey to replenish the Bear's supply.
They bathe in the stream and wash their dresses, dry
them in the sun. When they dress, Rose Red notices
that Rose White seems to be taking more care than
usual. Her hair is sunlight in sunlight. Her cheeks are
pink. She makes herself a wreath of wildflowers. She is
wearing the dress with the torn hem out of which she
made a bandage for the Bear.

Rose Red knows what is happening, a part of her
knows. She remembers what she and Rose White used
to say to each other when they were young. She touches
her hair—it feels coarse. She looks at her freckled arms
and her big strong calves. She looks at Rose White admiring herself in the stream, casting white petals over
her reflection.

The Bear is better that night. His breathing is more
regular and he eats more of the food they give him.
Rose Red builds a fire in the fireplace. She sees the

way the Bear stares at Rose White while she cleans and rebandages his wound. His eyes are full of dark firelight. Full of light and strength. Watching the Bear and Rose White, Rose Red feels the way she felt when she and Rose White first discovered the Bear—she can't breathe, her body seems to have frozen.

Days go by. Rose White and Rose Red spend them in the woods. Rose White's skin is glowing and her body seems to be filling out. Neither she nor Rose Red ever talk of leaving. At night they watch over the Bear.

One night it is especially cold. Rose Red wakes in the little bed with the carved headboard painted with blue hearts and yellow birds. Rose White is not there. Rose Red goes into the front room. The Bear is sleeping by the fireplace where he always sleeps. His wound has completely healed. His coat gleams. Rose White is curled up in the curve of his haunches. Rose Red stops breathing; she freezes. She knows that what Rose White told her once would now be a lie. She goes back to her bed and stares into the darkness where transformations are taking place.

In the morning when Rose Red comes in for break-

fast she sees a man sitting with Rose White at the little table with the blue-and-white-checked cloth. He is
tall and strong, with a shiny brush of brown hair and
fierce spellbinding brown eyes. He is staring at Rose
White, whose hair is like the honey sunlight pouring in
through the leaded glass window; she has berry-stained
lips and hands and is wearing her flower wreath and
her dress that is half the size it once was because it has
been turned mostly into bandages.

Rose White runs to Rose Red and kisses her with
her berry-stained lips. Rose Red swallows a trickle of
salt in her throat and smiles. She says, This is what is
supposed to happen, I'm so happy for you.

Rose White wants to tell her, maybe he has a friend,
you have to stay with us, things don't have to change
that much, but she doesn't say anything. She knows that
things have changed. When Rose Red sets out to leave
she holds his hand and lets her go.

Bones

I DREAMED OF BEING A PART OF THE STORIES—
even terrifying ones, even horror stories—because at
least the girls in stories were alive before they died.

My ears were always ringing from the music cranked
to pain-pitch in the clubs. Cigarette smoke perfumed my
hair, wove into my clothes. I took the occasional drug
when it came my way. The more mind-altering the
better. I had safe sex with boys I didn't know—usually
pretty safe. I felt immortal, which is how you are supposed to feel when you are young, I guess, no matter
what anybody older tells you. But I'm not sure I wanted
immortality that much then.

I met him at a party that a girl from my work told

me about. It was at this house in the hills, a small castle that some movie star had built in the fifties with turrets and balconies and balustrades. People were bringing of-ferings—bottles of booze and drugs and guitars and drums and paints and canvases. It was the real bohemian scene. I thought that in it I could become something else, that I could become an artist, alive. And everyone else wanted that, too; they were coming there for him.

Once he'd come into the restaurant late at night and I took his order but he didn't seem to notice me at all. I noticed him because of the color of his hair and goatee. I heard that he was this big promoter guy, managed bands, owned some clubs and galleries. A real patron of the arts, Renaissance man. Derrick Blue they called him, or just Blue. It was his house, his party, they were all making the pilgrimage for him.

It was summer and hot. I was sweating, worried my makeup would drip off. Raccoon pools of mascara and shadow around my eyes. The air had that grilled smell, meat and gasoline, that it gets in Los Angeles when the temperature soars. It was a little cooler in the house so I went in and sat on this overstuffed antique couch under some giant crimson painting of a girl's face with electric lights for her pupils, and drank my beer and watched everybody. There was a lot of posing going on, a kind of auditioning or something. More and more scantily clad girls kept coming, boys were playing music or drawing the girls or just lying back, smoking.

Derrick Blue came out after a while and he made the rounds—everybody upped the posing a little for him. I just watched. Then he came over and smiled and took my hand and looked into my eyes and how hungry I was, in every way. I was always hungry for food— blueberry pancakes and root beer floats and pizza gluey with cheese—I thought about it all the time. And other things. I'd sit around dreaming that the boys I saw at shows or at work—the boys with silver earrings and big boots—would tell me I was beautiful, take me home and feed me Thai food or omelets and undress me and make love to me all night with the palm trees whispering windsongs about a tortured, gleaming city and the moonlight like flame melting our candle bodies. And then I was hungry for him, this man who seemed to have everything, and to actually be looking at me. I didn't realize why he was looking.

He found out pretty fast that I wasn't from around there, didn't know too many people well, lived alone in a crummy hotel apartment in Koreatown, ate what I could take home from work. He knew how hungry I was. He asked everything as if he really cared and I just stared back at him and answered. He had blue eyes, so blue that they didn't dim next to his blue-dyed hair. Cold beveled eyes. They made the sweat on my temples evaporate and I felt like I was high on coke coke coke when he looked at me.

The crimson girl on the wall behind me, the girl with the open mouth and the bared teeth and the electric eyes, looked like she was smiling—until you looked closely.

Derrick Blue caught my arm as I was leaving—I was pretty drunk by then, the hillside was sliding and the flowers were blurry and glowy like in those 3-D postcards—and it was pretty late, and he said, stay. He said he wanted to talk to me, we could stay up all night talking and then have some breakfast. It was maybe two or three in the morning but the air was still hot like burning flowers. I felt sweat trickle down my ribs under my T-shirt.

We were all over his house. On the floor and the couches and tables and beds. He had music blasting from speakers everywhere and I let it take me like when I was at shows, thrashing around, losing the weight of who I was, the self-consciousness and anxiety, to the sound. He said, You're so tiny, like a doll, you look like you might break. I wanted him to break me. Part of me did. He said, I can make you whatever you want to be. I wanted him to. But what did I want to be? Maybe that was the danger.

The night was blue, like drowning in a cocktail. I tasted it bittersweet and felt the burning of ice on my skin. I reeled through the rooms of antiques and statues and huge-screen TVs and monster stereo systems and icy lights in frosted glass. If you asked me then if I would have died at that moment I might have said yes. What else was there? This was the closest thing to a story I'd ever known. Inside me it felt like nothing.

That night he told all the tales. You know, I am still grateful to him for that. I hadn't heard them since I

was little. They made me feel safe. Enchanted. Alive.
Charms. He said he had named himself for Bluebeard,
if I hadn't guessed. He said it had become a metaphor
for his whole life. He took a key from his pocket. I
wasn't afraid. I couldn't quite remember the story. I
felt the enchantment around us like stepping into a big
blue glitter storybook with a little mirror on the cover
and princesses dancing inside, dwarves and bears and
talking birds. And dying girls. He said, The key, it had
blood on it, remember? It was a fairy, and she couldn't
get the blood off, no matter what she did. It gave her
away. I knew that Bluebeard had done something terrible. I was starting to remember. When I first heard that
story I couldn't understand it—why is this a fairy tale?
Dead girls in a chamber, a psychotic killer with blue
hair. I tried to speak but the enchantment had seeped
into my mouth like choking electric blue frosting from
a cake. I looked up at him. I wondered how he managed it. If anyone came looking for the women. Not if
they were a bunch of lost girls without voices or love.
No one would have come then.

Part of me wanted to swoon into nothing, but the

other women's bones were talking. I didn't see the bones but I knew they were there, under the house. The little runaway bones of skinny, hungry girls who didn't think they were worth much—anything—so they stayed after the party was over and let Derrick Blue tell them his stories. He probably didn't even have to use much force on most of them.

I will rewrite the story of Bluebeard. The girl's brothers don't come to save her on horses, baring swords, full of power and at exactly the right moment. There are no brothers. There is no sister to call out a warning. There is only a slightly feral one-hundred-pound girl with choppy black hair, kohl-smeared eyes, torn jeans, and a pair of boots with steel toes. This girl has a little knife to slash with, a little pocket knife, and she can run. That is one thing about her—she has always been able to run. Fast. Not because she is strong or is running toward something but because she has learned to run away.

I pounded through the house, staggering down the

hallways, falling down the steps. It was a hot streaky
dawn full of insecticides, exhaust, flowers that could
make you sick or fall in love. My battered Impala was
still parked there on the side of the road and I opened it
and collapsed inside. I wanted to lie down on the shredded seats and sleep and sleep.

But I thought of the bones; I could hear them singing. They needed me to write their song.

Beast

BEAUTY'S FATHER THOUGHT THAT HE WAS through having children. His two daughters were a handful, running around the house, demanding that he look at them, compliment them. He didn't have much energy anymore. He was getting old, much older than his wife. Look at his wrinkles, look at his gray hair. What if he became ill and died before the baby was grown? But his wife convinced him—There's one more. Please. I feel her. Beauty's father said no; his wife insisted. She won. Soon after giving birth to Beauty, she was the one who got sick and died.

Beauty's father loved his youngest daughter, the child of his old age, more than anything in the world.

Maybe too much. After all, it was he who had named her. That was the first clue. It wasn't an easy name to have, no matter what you looked like. It predisposed her sisters to hate her from the beginning.

Not only was the name a bad choice; Beauty's father also picked the forbidden rose to bring to her. But it was necessary. Otherwise how would Beauty have met the Beast?

Beauty's father had to go away on a trip to purchase goods to sell in his store. He asked Beauty's sisters what they wanted, and they listed silk dresses with silver sari trim, pearled camisoles, lace nightgowns, ruby earrings, and French perfume. Beauty, who had her father's love and so didn't feel a need for much else, requested a single rose—she knew it would make him happy. This irritated her sisters to no end. They might even have asked for roses, too, if they had thought of it, and if it would have made their father love them more. But no, it was always Beauty who thought of those things first, making them look foolish and selfish. Well, it was too late. Now they would have their nice gifts, anyway. How could their father deny them? He would have felt too guilty, since they all knew whom he favored.

Beauty's father found the silk dresses with silver trim, the pearled camisoles, lace nightgowns, ruby earrings, and French perfume. He was going to wait until the last minute for the rose so that it would be fresh when he gave it to his daughter. But on the way home Beauty's father lost his way on a deserted road on a cliff between an ocean and a dark wood.

Then he saw a light, a melding rainbow light shining in the trees, and Beauty's father felt compelled to go to it. He walked through the pines and the redwood trees that towered above him. There were a few charred tree trunks blocking the paths; new, young trees grew out of these carcasses. He had read somewhere that when a redwood is burned it will be shocked into sprouting new greens from its roots so that a young tree will grow. Otherwise the baby tree would never have been born.

Pine needles and dead leaves slipped under his feet and he sank into dampness, branches catching at his clothes. His heart was beating at the root of his tongue and his hands were clammy but he kept on.

Beauty's father was relieved to come out of the forest. The house he had seen from the road was huge and made of stone. Each window was of stained glass, so that it almost resembled a cathedral. The garden surrounding the house was overflowing with flowering plants bathed in colored lights. The blossoms were the biggest, richest, and most succulent Beauty's father had ever seen. He knew that Beauty would love them.

Beauty's father walked up stone steps through the garden. The plants formed a bower, showering him with droplets of moisture and sweetening the air. He thought he heard music playing—light and tinkling and otherworldly.

The doors of the house opened as if by themselves, and Beauty's father felt the warmth from inside, heard the music more loudly now, saw a glow of light. He walked in.

There was a long hallway lit by torches in sconces in the shapes of outstretched arms. Trees grew up from the floor and out through the ceiling. Flowering vines grew over all the furniture. There were many low cushions in soft, luxurious though somewhat worn fabrics. Everywhere was a comfortable, warm corner to curl up in.

Beauty's father smelled delectable food wafting through the rooms. He followed the scent to a dining area with a low table and more cushions. Torches burned. On the table was a feast. Platters of steaming, seasoned meats, vegetables, and grains made Beauty's father salivate like an animal. There were no utensils but when he saw the little sign telling him to Please Eat, he didn't hesitate to voraciously lap everything up.

Afterward, Beauty's father lay back on the cushions. He closed his eyes and fell asleep.

When he woke he began to explore. He came to a courtyard garden where the flowers were even bigger and more lavish than the ones he had seen in front of the house.

That was when Beauty's father noticed the rose. The rose that proved he loved his daughter too much. There was a little sign in front of it that read, Please Do Not Pick the Flowers.

The rose reminded him of his daughter—open, glowing, pink and white, fragrant. Did he know it reminded him of her because it was forbidden? He only knew he had to have it. It looked fresh enough to last for days and he wasn't that far from home—he could keep it in a jar of water.

But when he leaned to pluck it the inevitable happened. Didn't he realize? How often has this been told?

The Beast came out of the shadows, lumbering on his four legs, his four weighty paws; his glossy black coat moving liquidly over his muscular body, his huge, heavy head swaying slightly, the squareness of it, his big jaw to hold his sharp teeth. All of this distracted Beauty's father so much, of course, that he did not look into the Beast's eyes. If he had, he might not have been afraid. Or maybe, more so? The Beast's eyes were the dark, slightly slanted, loving, fierce, hypnotizing eyes of a god.

You take the one thing that you are not allowed to touch? growled the Beast. You have insulted me and my hospitality.

Beauty's father apologized, wondering what had been in the food. What kind of dream was this? And how could he wake up?

The Beast stalked around Beauty's father in circles,

like a nightmare, his head slung low between his shoulder blades, the hairs on his back standing up.

Beauty's father tried to explain, mumbled something about his daughter, Beauty, how all she wanted was a rose, he loved her, wasn't thinking, had never seen flowers like that, never seen . . .

After what seemed like a very long time, the Beast told Beauty's father that he could go. On one condition.

This was the part Beauty's father somehow knew. He began to shake his head, no, not that, anything else. The Beast said it was the only way. Beauty's father must obey, otherwise when he returned home he would become very ill and die.

Beauty's father left the Beast's home, running down the stone corridors where the hands holding torches seemed to reach out to burn him, staggering out the heavy door through the garden that now smelled suffocating, into the dark forest that was now comforting. He saw a faint light at the edge of the sky and knew it would be day soon—he could find someone to take him to the nearest town. He was alive, he had had a terrible dream.

But in his hand was the rose.

Beauty's father returned home with the gifts for his daughters. The two older ones weren't particularly impressed—this was because they knew his love for them was not bleeding in the rubies or anywhere else. Only Beauty expressed delight. She kissed his hands, thanking him. His hands that were covered with pale brown spots and thick blue veins. His hands that had comforted and protected her since she was born, a child of his old age whom he thought he would never see grow into womanhood. She knew how precious the rose gift was. It was a sign of his devotion, and, ultimately, a release from it.

A few days after he'd returned home, Beauty's father became ill. Beauty put him to bed where she fed and bathed him. He had glass eyes and parchment lips. His skin burned with a mysterious fever. Beauty asked him what was wrong over and over again. She sensed he was hiding something from her. What was it? Had he been to a doctor and found something? Why wouldn't he go see one now? Beauty's father finally admitted that something strange had happened to him on his trip. He wouldn't say more but one night, in a dream, he spoke out loud about the Beast and the rose, and Beauty heard. She made him tell her when he woke up.

After Beauty's father had told her the story, he regretted it and tried to say it was just delirium from the fever. But she was too wise for that. Besides, secretly, without even knowing it herself, she had been waiting for a Beast to go to.

Because of this, it was easier than it might have sounded for Beauty to go to the Beast. She would not listen to her father's pleas; she had made up her mind. It was the first time she had ever disobeyed him.

Beauty rode along the coast, marveling at the changing colors of the ocean, the sea lions she saw sleeping on the sand like shifting black rocks, the formations of birds writing poetry in the sky, zebra grazing in a field among some cows and horses. She sang to herself and let the wind tangle her hair. She had never felt so free. This was the right thing, she knew.

But then she got to the wood and saw the house and she became afraid. She had had so little time to feel herself, without the weight of her sisters' jealousy, her father's love. She wanted more wind and sea and zebras. Now she was going into another locked place.

Still, she had made her promise. So she walked through the garden filled with tempting flowers, and through the doors that opened as she approached them, down the hallway lit with torches. She sat on a cushion in front of a low table that was spread with foods she had never seen or even heard of before. There were translucent sweet red and green fruits shaped like hearts, bright gold roasted-tasting grains shaped like stars, huge ruffley purple vegetables and small satiny blue ones. Everything smelled fresh and rich and light, and Beauty found herself stooped over her plate, licking it, like a wild animal. She ate until she was too full to move and then she lay back on the cushions and fell asleep.

When she woke, the candles had burned down to lumpy puddles of wax, and she had been undressed and tucked into a bed made from the cushions. She sat up, holding her arms over her chest. Who had done this? Why hadn't she heard or felt him? Where was he now?

As if in answer the Beast came out from behind a curtain and sat down on his haunches before her, looking at her with those slanted dark eyes. She could not look away.

Did you undress me? she asked.

The Beast nodded his huge head. He looked so gentle and kind that she didn't know what to say next. She wanted to stroke his fur and scratch his ears until he cocked his head and rumbled his throat with pleasure. She wanted to get up and run with him through the woods until they fell down weak and panting with exhaustion. She wanted to lie against his warm, heaving side and sleep.

And this was just what happened. For the next few weeks Beauty and her companion never spoke. He knew her thoughts and tried to give her everything she needed. Even more—he seemed to feel her feelings. When she was sad he moaned softly in his sleep, then woke to nuzzle his cool nose against her neck. When she was happy he frisked around her, wagging and wiggling with joy like a pup. They ate together at the low table and ran together through the woods. The Beast showed Beauty secret pathways and how to hear sounds that had once been hidden from her, how to read the scents among the foliage—who had been there, what they desired, where they had gone. When the smells were evil the Beast became wild, baring his teeth, grabbing Beauty's dress in his teeth, practically dragging her back with him to the house. She was never afraid, though, not with the Beast beside her, not with what he had taught her.

Beauty began to change. Her hair was always a tangle, she bathed less often, her skin smelled of the garden and the forest, she was almost always barefoot—there were hard calluses on her soles. Her senses were so sharp that she could smell and hear things she had never known existed before. This was the happiest she had ever been in her life, if happiness is waking with a start of joy for the day, feeling each moment in every cell of your being, and going to sleep at night with a mind like a clear moonlit sky.

Beauty was never overwhelmed or suffocated by the Beast's love, even though, when she left him alone, even for a short time, he looked as if his heart was literally cracking in half inside his chest. But he understood freedom, her Beast. He understood shackles. He never wanted her to feel chains around her neck as he had once felt them. But now she had become his chain in a strange way, and he knew it.

When Beauty called her father that first night he heard the light and air in her daughter's voice and almost immediately he was better. It was as if the guilt he had carried for so long about his wife's death (had he loved his youngest daughter too much, is that why she died?), the neglect of his other daughters, his blind, panicky obsession with Beauty that had driven him to pick the rose that now imprisoned her—because he had told her about it!—was all gone now.

But after a few weeks, he began to long for her again—just to see her face. He knew he was going to die soon. Please come back home, he begged her. Just for a little while.

Beauty asked the Beast. He lay his heavy, warm, silky head in her lap and gazed up at her. How could he deny her anything? He felt her need to see her father in his own heart as only Beasts can.

So Beauty left him and went home. Her father was startled at how his Beauty had changed. He asked again and again if she was sure she was all right, was the Beast hurting her in any way? No, she reassured him. She was happy. Her sisters were horrified. They thought she looked hideous—what was she doing out there in the woods? Beauty smiled at them and shook her matted locks and tried to restrain herself from licking her hand as if it were a paw.

Beauty sat by her father's side and held his hand and spoke softly but all she was thinking about, really, was her Beast. How they didn't need words. How ferocious he became if he ever thought she was in danger. How gentle he was, licking her nose; no one in the world could be so gentle. How she had become so different since she had been with him, so much stronger—she could run for hours now—so much more perceptive and tangled, and how she slept so much better and ate so much more.

Every night before she went to sleep she sent him messages and received his. This was not hard to do—he had taught her about communicating without words.

But each time a message came, Beauty felt his sadness growing deeper, so painful that she wasn't sure which of their emotions she was feeling, his or hers. It was like a sickness and she sent him the message that she would return to him as soon as possible, but not yet, her father still needed her.

After Beauty's father died, she wept. But she also felt a strange sense of relief. The relief frightened her. She went back to her Beast. He was lying by the cold fireplace, with his head down; he was too weak to stand. His eyes were blank, his coat was dull and sparse, his bones stuck out. He looked as if he were dying. Beauty was shocked that she had been so wrong not to see, not to come to him sooner. She was so shocked by his pain that she didn't even notice the biggest change of all that came about when she threw her arms around him and told him again and again that she loved him more than anyone in the world, she would never love anyone else in such a pure, vast way.

Yes, the Beast changed.

He spoke more now, and did not gaze at Beauty in the same intense, almost pained way, as if he were feeling every emotion she felt. He did not sigh in his sleep when she sighed and his stomach didn't growl when hers hurt. He could not read her thoughts anymore, and she could not read his. He seemed a bit more clumsy and guarded and distant, too. They no longer ran through the woods together, although they still walked there sometimes. They quarreled and raised their voices to each other once in a while. Each time, after they quarreled, Beauty bathed, combed the tangles from her hair, and began to wear shoes again for a few days.

Beauty loved him more than anything, her Beast boy, but, secretly, sometimes, she wished that he would have remained a Beast.

Ice

SHE CAME THAT NIGHT LIKE EVERY GIRL'S WORST
fear, dazzling frost star ice queen. Tall and with that
long silver blond hair and a flawless face, a perfect
body in white crushed velvet and a diamond snowflake
tiara. The boys and girls parted to let her through—
they had all instantaneously given up on him when
they saw her.

I felt almost—relieved. Like that first night with
him but different. Relieved because what I dreaded
most in the whole world was going to happen and I
wouldn't have to live with it anymore—the fear.

There is the relief of finally not being alone and the
relief of being alone when no one can take anything

away from you. Here she was, my beautiful fear. Shiny
as crystal lace frost.

I loved him the way it feels when you get hot wax
on the inside of your wrist and while it's burning, just
as sudden, it's a cool thick skin. Like it tastes to eat
sweet snow, above the daffodil bulbs—not that I've ever
found it, but clean snow that melts to nothing on the
heat of your tongue so that you aren't even sure if it
was ever there. I loved him like spaniel joy at a scent in
the grass—riveted, lost. I loved him so much that it felt
as if it had to be taken away from me at any moment,
changed—how could something like that be allowed to
exist on this earth?

We lived in apartments that faced each other and
sometimes I'd look up when I was painting and I'd see
him watching me but then he'd look away. I watched
him, too, when he was practicing his guitar sometimes.
We nodded when we saw each other in the street but
we never spoke.

I went to the Mirror one night by myself and when
I heard him sing I could feel everything he was feeling.
I could feel the throb in the ankle he'd twisted jumping

into the pit a couple of nights before, the way the sweat was trickling down his temples, making them itch, the way his throat felt a little bit scratchy and sore and how he wanted to go away from that smoky room, drive out to the lake for some air, how there was something from his childhood that he was trying to forget by singing but how it never quite left him—though I couldn't quite feel what it was. I have felt people before; my mom used to call me an empath. When she got sick I developed lumps in my breasts and my hair was falling out for a while. It only happened with people I loved, though. Never a stranger. Never a singing stranger with golden hair tousled in his face and deep-set blue eyes and a big Adam's apple. Maybe my empathy was just because of him. He could make you feel things. Maybe every person in that room was feeling what he did.

But this was what was strange—he knew me, too. He gazed down through the smoke and kept looking at me while he sang about the shard of glass in his eye. Trying to melt it away. Tears. But he was dry. When it was over I felt like I'd been kissed for hours all over my body. I could feel my own tears running down my cheeks and neck.

I felt small and stupid-looking and bald when it was over, when I came back to my body and my shorn head. I wanted to go and hide from him. But he found me. He came walking through the crowd and smoke and everyone was trying to talk to him or touch him and he looked wiped out. He looked like he had given every single thing and what could they want from him now? His eyes looked bigger and more hollowly set and I could feel his sore throat and his dry burning glass-stung eyes. He came up to me and sat down and he asked right then if I wanted to get out of there with him, if I wanted to go get high or whatever, he had to get out right now he liked the tattoo of the rose on the inside of my wrist. He didn't say anything about recognizing me from before.

The streets were slick with frost, my fingers and nose and toes went numb, my toes knocking against my boots with hammering pain. I didn't care. I watched him light a cigarette, holding it in his hand with the fingerless mittens, cupping the flame, protecting it, handing it to me, lighting another for himself. He said

he thought smoking was a primitive reflex to the cold—
like building fires. The cold inside, too. Our boots
crunched through thin sheets of ice. I thought that if I
were still crying my tears would freeze and I could give
them to him—icicles to suck on. But he needed warming, to be kissed with the fire of a thousand cigarettes.

We walked for a while and then he got a cab and
we went to his place. That's when he said he hoped I
didn't mind, that he'd been watching me through the
window, he wasn't a crazy stalker or anything, he just
couldn't help it. He said not to take this the wrong way
but I reminded him of a sister. He said he believed
in that thing about everyone having another half out
there, like a twin, that you were supposed to find and
that almost no one ever did. We sat in the room that
I'd seen through glass for so long, the room with the
mattress and the music and the thrift shop lamps and
we got high and talked all night. Mostly I did; I told
him about my mom and he just listened, but he kept
thanking me for telling him. It was almost as if hearing
it was as much a relief for him as my saying it. We both
kept saying how relieved we felt—relieved, that was the

word we kept using. I was like an accident victim who's been rescued, pulled breathing from the wreckage—until I began to feel afraid.

All that winter I painted him with his eyes like moons or his head crowned with stars or a frozen city melting in his hands. I had some ideas of how I was going to paint him riding on the back of a reindeer, eating snowflakes, holding a swan. He wrote songs about a girl who was a storm, a fire, a mirror. My hair grew out and I started wearing sparkling light-colored soft soft things I'd found in thrift shops. I had a fake fur coat and a pastel sequin shirt and rhinestones. We got the flu and ate rice balls and miso soup in the bathtub. I gave him vitamin C and echinacea. He felt better. We went to the Mirror and he always made sure to find me right after he sang and hold me so no one else would try to touch him. He knew I was afraid that somehow he would be taken away from me. I never said it but I knew he knew that was why I cried at night, sometimes, after we had made the sheets so hot I was afraid they would stick to our skin like melted wax. He told me over and over again, The songs are for you, you are the girl in the songs, you are all I think about when I pull you into the vortex of our bodies. I never really believed him. Is that why it happened? Because I never believed a real love which then felt betrayed? Or was it because I had sensed something true all along?

Maybe it happened because when he was sad I tried to get him to remember. I asked what it was he was trying to forget. I said that for me, pain lessened when you let it out, shared it. He shook his head, slid farther away. Maybe I was just being selfish, wanting to know his secret, whatever it was, the one thing he wouldn't let me have.

Spring came. We planted flowers in our window boxes since we didn't have gardens. One morning when we woke up we saw that the tendrils had twisted together, across the space between our windows.

I painted him with flocks of birds circling, opaled wings spreading out of his back, flowers blooming full burst from his mouth. He wrote songs about a girl who was a fish, a light, a rose. He held me every night, his sweat dripping off onto me, his eyes glazed, my throat aching from the strain of his vocal cords. He said he got

so tired. That I was the only thing that could restore
him. Boys and girls wanted more than just the songs.
They wanted to touch him, they wanted to feel what he
was feeling after the songs were over, they wanted him
to feel them. I took him home with me. We sat curled
in my velvet love seat; he held my wrist, asking ques-
tions, and I told him what had happened to me. I tried
to get him to tell me what hurt him but then he became
even more silent.

He began to have trouble writing songs. He looked
blurry to me after he sang. He was fading, I was sure
of it. Just this blur of gold light. He said he didn't know
what people wanted anymore. After a while I couldn't
give him himself back after he sang, no matter what I
did. I lay awake at night watching him sleep—his eyelashes tipped with gold, the rise and fall of his chest—
thinking, any day now, this can't last. Look at him. He
is too perfect. Like an angel carved on a tomb. If you try
to keep something so perfect, you get only silent stone.

And then winter again.

That was when she came, my beautiful fear. My fear
so beautiful that I almost desired it—her. She was the

porn goddess, ice sex, glistening and shiny and perfection. Something you wanted to eat and wear and own and be. Something poisonous delicious forbidden.

She went straight for him and he couldn't fight her and I didn't hate him. I just vanished. With my little less-bald-than-it-had-been head and my fuzzy coat and my big boots against which my numb toes would slam. He didn't find me after the show and I was no longer the storm girl, fish girl, rose girl, mirror. I was nothing and she was everything and he was gone.

Later, he saw the rose tattooed on my wrist, and he said, Why did you get that there? The tattoo he had loved the first night we touched. And I said, I told you, remember? I covered some scars when I tried to cut myself after my mom died and he said, I don't know if I can handle this, and turned away. She had changed him. The ice was in his eye and in his heart, like he had predicted with that song, but now they were deep embedded there, all the pain of the world. Not pain to make you feel for somebody else but pain to make you stop feeling.

I would have ridden on a reindeer or the back of a

bird, I would have gone to the North Pole and I would have woven a blanket out of the threads of my body. I would have ripped out my hair and had implanted a wig of long silver blond strands, cut my body and sewn on whole new parts. I would have flayed my skin to find a more perfect whiteness beneath. I would have given him my eyes or my heart so that I could live in him, lying in her arms. At least then I could be close to him. These are the things of stories and I couldn't do any of them. All I could do was go back to my room and pull down the blinds and paint.

I painted every story about stolen deadened boys, nearly devoured by evil queens, revived by loving girls. I painted myself ripping out my hair, cutting off parts of me, sewing on new ones. I painted myself on the back of a reindeer. Fish girl storm girl mirror girl. But sometimes art can't save you. It had before I met him but now it couldn't. I painted myself and my twin melding into one and eaten by the ice. I was dying but inside him I lived. What would happen to me if she took his soul forever? He is lying in her burning cold bed watching the video screen. This is how they touch. She's too perfect to be real. He touches himself looking at her. Parts of him are dying and he is blissful. Why did he need to feel things for so long? Look where it got him. Hungry hungry boys and girls who would collect pieces of him if they could to put in their beds, scrapbooks, boxes, put on their plates. A twin who wept almost every night thinking she would lose him. He can't do this to her. It's better this way. Poor insecure little bald girl. Remember walking through the frost? Remember her paintings that he said were how things should really look? The flowers tangling into each other? No, he's forgotten. The Ice Queen is undressing for him again.

I'll make you a god, she said.

That's what I heard. At the Mirror, in the streets. She said, Move in with me. I'll give you anything you want. How could he refuse? Me crying on the phone. Or her. And everything. It wasn't much of a choice.

Then he disappeared.

She was alone at the Mirror, surrounded by girls and boys who looked ready to lap her up like walking candy. Where is K.? they asked. She just smiled. So pretty it could blind you. Snowflakes in the sun.

Rumors started that he was dead. OD'd. Gun to the skull. She was a killer, you could see it. Someone should go check it out.

But the boys and girls were being fed on her. She started performing for them. They forgot about him.

I'd stare into his dark, empty apartment and see him in the window playing his guitar, dancing around like a puppet with his hair in his face. My beautiful boy. He'd stop, look up, shake away his hair, look across at me with his shadowy eyes. But he wasn't there at all.

A bird landed on my flower box. I asked it had it seen him? The bird said, Ask the flowers. All the ones he and I had planted had died. I walked down by the lake where we used to go. Some roses were struggling up. I asked them. They said they'd been under the ground and he wasn't there. They said I should go to see her.

She lived in a house high above the city and ice was on the ground. Everywhere else it had started to melt. The numb pain came back in my toes and fingers. I walked through the iron gates, up the icy path among the snow-covered trees, over the threshold of the white palace. The floors were cold marble and echoing. Everything was white. The chill was so harsh that I could see my breath, even inside. I went looking for him.

Up white marble stairs into a white marble room decorated with giant crystal snowflakes hanging from the ceiling, catching-refracting the light. He lay sleeping at her feet in a little lump. He was barefoot and his feet looked so cold. The blue veins stood out, vulnerable. I wanted to warm his feet in my armpits but I was cold too. She was even more beautiful than I remembered her. I thought that I had made a mistake. There was no way he could love me after seeing her even just once.

But at least I could touch him again, wake him, something. See if he was still alive inside. Then I'd leave.

She said I really shouldn't come barging in like that, didn't I know he didn't want me anymore? She touched her hair and light leaped off of it like diamonds. She touched her throat and I felt mine close with fear.

I remembered how love is supposed to break evil spells. Only if you love purely. I understood how he had come to her. He wanted something that could make him forget. There was something bad enough inside him that he had to forget and I couldn't help him. I always wanted to remember, wanted him to remember.

But now I thought that if he opened his eyes I would leave, never come back to bother him again. I just had to see if he was all right. Maybe I could tell him that I understood about forgetting.

I knelt beside him and put my hands on his cheekbones. His neck was limp. I breathed on his face, whispering his name. My breath made a cloud and it melted the icicles on his eyelashes. I said, Come back here. I just want to see if you're okay. Then I'll leave if you want. I promise, I'll leave.

She was watching us, amused, I think. She stood up and stretched languidly and slipped off her white satin gown and waited there naked, burning white and not shivering at all in the chill air. She was so beautiful that I thought I had really gone mad this time, even trying to get him to look at me.

My tears were so hot that they didn't freeze on my cheeks. They poured off of me onto him. They splashed on his upturned face. They poured over his eyelids, dripped into his eyes, seeped into him. I wanted them to wash away the particles of glass.

He looked up at me. He seemed to have shrunken, gotten even paler. He said my name. I wanted to drag him away, covering his eyes, but instead I let him see her there, behind us. Naked and glistening. He stared and I could feel his palm start to sweat, his heart beat fast like it was going to jump into her. I wanted to die, then. I wanted to destroy the body I was trapped in, become what she was, no matter what it took. No matter how much mutilation or pain. But he looked away, at me. He pulled my face down and pressed my lips against his like he was almost trying to suffocate us both.

Once he and I were children, before this happened.

More titles by Francesca Lia Block!

Francesca Lia Block is a master at the art of lyrical storytelling. Written in spare, poetic prose, Block's characters explore both the magic and the hard realities of her vividly depicted urban landscapes. She has described her work as "contemporary fairy tales with an edge," where the real world finds solace for its troubles through "hope and magic."